Oedipus The Teacher

OEDIPUS THE TEACHER

A Return to Thebes

Kalman J. Kaplan

FOREWORD BY
Matthew B. Schwartz

RESOURCE *Publications* • Eugene, Oregon

OEDIPUS THE TEACHER
A Return to Thebes

Resource Publications
An Imprint of Wipf and Stock Publishers
199 W. 8th Ave., Suite 3
Eugene, OR 97401

www.wipfandstock.com

PAPERBACK ISBN: 978-1-5326-8659-7
HARDCOVER ISBN: 978-1-5326-8660-3
EBOOK ISBN: 978-1-5326-8661-0

Manufactured in the U.S.A.

Dedication

Again, to my parents, Lewis C. Kaplan and Edith Saposnik Kaplan, both authors/translators in their own life who raised me with the self-confidence to follow my own path, to Moriah Markus-Kaplan, a fellow psychologist who has provided hospitality in Israel to further my understanding of Biblical versus Greek ways of thinking, and to my son Daniel Lewis Kaplan, also a psychologist whom I often pestered if not bombarded with my insights in this regard when he was growing up. I hope my descendants will find this play useful in their thinking and in their lives and help them cope with any setbacks they may face rather than catastrophize them. Much of so-called modern "higher education" has explicitly or implicitly bought into the ancient Greek tragic view of life, and tends to dismiss people with a biblical outlook. This view is condescending in the extreme and often quite shallow. I wish to instill in my descendants the biblical sense that people can overcome adversity, which everyone faces at one time or another, and go on to live inherently meaningful lives.

Acknowledgements

The Author would like to acknowledge the comments and insights provided by Dr. Michael Shapiro, Dr. Daniel Silverfarb, Dr. Lori Thomson, Dr. Matthew Schwartz and Isabelle Proton, Esq. The author must also acknowledge Sophocles' great trilogy, *Oedipus the King, Oedipus at Colonus and Antigone*. We have abridged small passages of dialogue from the translations from the Greek presented in respective translations in W. S. Oates and E. O'Neill, Jr., 1938, *The Complete Greek Tragedy, Volume 1*, New York: Random House, from the narrative of the death of Zeno the Stoic in Diogenes Laertius, 1972, *The Lives of Eminent Philosophers*, Translated by Robert D. Hicks, Cambridge, MA: Harvard University Press, from Hesiod, 1991, *The Works and Days, Theogony, The Shield of Heracles*, Translated by Richard Lattimore, Ann Arbor, MI: The University of Michigan Press, Herodotus, 1961 *Histories*, Translated by Aubrey de Selincourt,. Baltimore, MD: Penguin Book, Smith, B. Sidney, 10 Apr 2014. Zeno's Paradox of the Tortoise and Achilles. *Platonic Realms Interactive Mathematics Encyclopedia*: http://platonicrealms.com/encyclopedia/ Zeno's-Paradox-of-the-Tortoise-and-Achilles, and from *Oxford Classical Dictionary, The*, 1970, edited by M. G. L. Hammond and H. H. Scullard. Second Edition. Oxford, England: Oxford at the Clarendon Press.

We have also paraphrased small passages regarding Job, Samson, Abraham and Isaac, and Ruth and Naomi, and Noah contained in *The Holy Scriptures*, 1955, Philadelphia, PA: The Jewish Publication Society of America, and also passages from the *Babylonian Talmud*, (1975) Vilna Edition.

Foreword

IN THE INITIAL PLAY in this trilogy, *Oedipus in Jerusalem*, Dr. Kalman Kaplan, a Professor of Clinical Psychology, presents us with a two-act play built upon the frame of a work by Sophocles. The latter was a famed Greek playwright of the fifth century BCE. In fact, he lived for almost that entire century. His fame lay both in his remarkably positive civic service and accomplishments, and also in the fact that he won more prizes than the other dramatists of his time, including Aeschylus and Euripides. These three frequently competed for the prize at the annual Athenian festivals. Sophocles wrote 123 plays for the competition. The first time Sophocles won was in 468 BCE, when he defeated Aeschylus for the prize.

The most famous of Sophocles' works is *Oedipus the King*. In his play, Oedipus is caught in the trap set by the fateful gods, unwittingly killing his father and committing incest with his mother. Upon discovering the truth, he blinds himself and wants to kill himself for being part of such an accursed family. He is confined to the palace, against his will, until the oracles can be consulted, though they have driven him to this tragic destiny by their messages of blind fate.

Kaplan redesigns the structure of Sophocles' play, presenting the play with a new story line, plot, thrust and denouement. The characters essentially remain the same, but for the addition of the Hebrew prophet, Nathan, of biblical note, who brings Oedipus, the fated king, to Jerusalem for a trial by the Sanhedrin. Here the intrigue and tension of the play elevates and accelerates. As the courtroom drama adds new dimensions to the original play, Oedipus in Jerusalem, takes on a stirring twist. Kaplan's whole intent is to set in tension and contrast not only two perspectives on Oedipus' destiny, but the dramatic difference between two world-views, Greek and Hebrew, in the ancient world and ours today. This involves comparing the theologies about the nature of God, codes of justice, methods of juridical procedure and, especially, comprehensive world-views both in the ancient world and the world today.

The play is set against the backdrop of a long cultural history. The historic Greek philosophical world-view is famous for such figures as Pythagoras, Plato, Aristotle, the Sophists, the Epicureans, and even Philo Judaeus, Plotinus, and Porphyry. Historically, that cultural history boiled down to the idealism of Platonism and the practical empiricism of Aristotelianism. These world views largely shaped the world from the fifth century BCE to our own time. Kaplan sets this world-view over against the trial of Oedipus in Jerusalem. The outcome is a twist, a surprise, a definitive destiny that the entire chaotic world must take account of in our day. Kaplan brings a piece of history to the table that we must pay attention to, at the risk of fate and the disaster of a self-fulfilling prophecy, facing us this very minute.

The Rev. Dr. J. Harold Ellens

Kalman Kaplan presents his *Oedipus Redeemed* as a sequel to his striking *Oedipus in Jerusalem*. Is the tragic nature of Classic Greek society actually redeemable or will it move only and inevitably toward self-destruction, as with so many of its heroes? The sages of Jerusalem led by Nathan the Prophet guide the self-blinded Oedipus from a potential tragic denouement toward a possibility of redemption. Insight is offered as an alternative to sight per se. Oedipus entering Colonus is portrayed by Sophocles as going to a tragic death. Oedipus entering the very different air of Jerusalem can still find acceptance from God and even from his family as he is reunited with his daughter Ismene whom he thought was lost to him.

Matthew B. Schwartz, Ph.D.

In *Oedipus the Teacher*, Professor Kalman Kaplan has brought forth the third entry in his new Oedipus trilogy. We see that the Oedipus story did not have to end in utter tragic destruction, as did Sophocles' version. Oedipus's experience in Jerusalem has taught him the value of hope which supplies a positive denouement to the seeming tragedy of Oedipus's earlier years. His hardships both self-inflicted and fated, provoked and then exacerbated by misleading riddles, are transformed as Oedipus takes on the role of teacher in Thebes and tries to help others benefit from his experiences in Jerusalem. Tragedy is absorbed into teaching and combated. The play portrays how Oedipus learns to teach utilizing parables and how he handles this new and most important role. An important side plot is the reconciliation of Oedipus with his surviving daughter Ismene, who is torn between her feelings for her father and her growing love for young Kallias. In loving one can she love the other as well? Again, the characters are turned to a Biblical model to understand how she indeed can love both, and Oedipus lives on to teach the grandson that is the fruit of Ismene's marriage. Important issues are raised about how to teach as Oedipus adjusts to his finally happy aging.

Matthew B. Schwartz, Ph.D.

In Memorial

The author would like to honor the memory of J. Harold Ellens who wrote the forward to the first play in this trilogy, *Oedipus in Jerusalem*. Hal Ellens was a learned and kind human being and a wonderful and prolific colleague. He died peacefully at home with his family in Farmington Hills, Michigan on April 13, 2018.

Preface

IN THE FIRST PLAY of this trilogy, *Oedipus in Jerusalem*, the biblical prophet Nathan meets the blind Oedipus wandering alone outside of Thebes, insisting that he is the worst person who ever lived. Convinced that Oedipus has been entrapped by misleading information, Nathan brings him to Jerusalem to be tried at the Jewish Sanhedrin. The Greek playwright Sophocles is the prosecutor and Nathan serves as the defense attorney. Oedipus is acquitted of the charges of patricide and incest but refuses to accept the court's decision.

Oedipus Redeemed describes the attempts by Nathan and Sophocles to accept his acquittal, ending with the Greek Oedipus returning to the Jewish Sanhedrin (High Court) in Jerusalem where he agrees to try to accept emotionally the acquittal he has received with regard to intentionally killing his father and marrying his mother, something he had rejected at the end of the first play of this trilogy, *Oedipus in Jerusalem*.

In this third play of this cycle, *Oedipus the Teacher*, Oedipus returns to Thebes with his one surviving daughter Ismene and an assistant, Kallias, son of the playwright Theodectes who has been recruited by Sophocles. Meanwhile Nathan and Sophocles travel to Corinth together and then to Delphi and then to Thebes. They discuss the life of young Oedipus in Corinth, and his sudden journey to the Oracle at Delphi (the Pythia), and the entire process of consulting with the Pythia who transmitted her responses to his questions in riddles.

They suggest several destructive riddles emergent in Greek culture. First, the riddle presented to Croesus, the king of Lydia; second, a riddle deciphered by the Athenian leader, Themistocles;

third, Zeno of Elea's construction of the paradox of the race between Achilles and the tortoise, and finally, *Homer's Riddle* illustrating how Homer's preoccupation with a children's riddle leads to a lack of attention to his actual physical surrounds and his death.

In the second act, Oedipus begins to teach a class of young Thebans headed by Alec. Oedipus tells of what he has learned in his time in Jerusalem regarding free will as opposed to fatalism (the Greek "moira"), and the danger of riddles outlined above as opposed to biblical parables. This is complicated by his initially supportive assistant Kallias falling in love with Ismene and becoming rivalrous towards Oedipus, who Kallias sees as blocking the possibility of his marriage to Ismene. Kallias does not come to the next class where Oedipus discusses the story of Samson and of how following one's eyes can lead one astray. Sophocles and Nathan invite the Greek chronicler Hesiod and the biblical prophetess, Deborah to the subsequent class.

Hesiod discusses the story in his *Theogony* of Cronus cutting off his father Uranus's genitals. The prophetess and judge Deborah, in turn, discusses the story of Abraham circumcising his son Isaac and God staying Abraham's hand on Mount Moriah as Abraham is about to sacrifice Isaac. Deborah also tells the story of Boaz and Ruth taking the aging Naomi into their home. This leads to a reconciliation between Kallias and Oedipus, acceptance by Oedipus of Ismene's marriage to Kallias, and the taking of Oedipus into their home. Ismene gives birth to a son, Jason, whom Oedipus dotes over, introducing him to a Greek translation of the Hebrew Scriptures. The play ends with Kallias and Alec excitedly announcing that Oedipus's course has been chosen to be taught in Thebes and the surrounding area, and indeed all over Greece.

Characters

Nasi (President of the Sanhedrin)

Av Bet Din (Vice-President of the Sanhedrin)

Spokesman for the Sanhedrin

Oedipus

Nathan, biblical prophet and defender of Oedipus

Sophocles, Greek playwright and previous accuser of Oedipus

Ismene, daughter of Oedipus

Kallias, young Theban who becomes an assistant of Oedipus in the teaching of his class

Alec, leader of and spokesman for the twelve Theban students of Oedipus

The other eleven Theban students.

Hesiod, Greek chronicler

Deborah, biblical prophetess

Jason, the young son of Kallias and Ismene and grandson of Oedipus

Acts And Scenes

Act II: Oedipus Teaches (and Learns) | 43

Scene II-14. The continuation of the past class begins the following week. Both Oedipus and Kallias expresses their fear of being abandoned. Deborah first tells Ismene, Kallias and Oedipus and the entire class the biblical story of Solomon determining which of two women was the mother of a dead infant, and which of a live infant. Oedipus and Kallias begin to reconcile after hearing this story. Deborah then tells Ismene, Kallias and Oedipus the biblical story of Ruth bringing her widowed mother-in-law Naomi into her home with her new husband Boaz and their son Obed. Oedipus and Kallias fully reconcile and Oedipus gives his blessing for the wedding of Kallias and Ismene. They invite him to live in their home. The biblical story of God putting a rainbow in the sky after the great flood is celebrated as a symbol of hope and as an antidote to the Greek story of the first woman Pandora locking hope up in the urn given to her by Zeus after loosing all the evils into the world. They all celebrate. | 110

Scene II-15. Five years later Ismene has married Kallias and Oedipus lives with them. She has given birth to a son, Jason, who is now four years old and whom Oedipus dotes over. Sophocles, Kallias and Alex arrive and announce that Oedipus's course will become part of the standard curriculum for all students of Thebes and adjoining cities in Greece. | 121

Act I: A Return To Thebes

Scene I-1. A revisit to the Sanhedrin.

The Sanhedrin in Jerusalem is reconvened. OEDIPUS returns with NATHAN, SOPHOCLES and his daughter ISMENE.

NASI (President of the Sanhedrin): I have received a request from both Nathan and Sophocles to reopen the proceedings of your trial, Oedipus. Is this correct?

NATHAN (interjecting): Yes, *Adoni*, we want to reopen the proceedings regarding Oedipus.

NASI: This is most unusual. Oedipus has already been acquitted of the charges Sophocles brought against him. What is his complaint?

AV BET DIN (Vice-President of the Sanhedrin): He did not accept his acquittal.

NASI: This is most unusual. Why would someone not accept a verdict of not guilty?

NATHAN: Because Oedipus insisted he was guilty.

NASI: But we reasoned he was entrapped by the Pythia. (to the SPOKESMAN FOR THE SANHEDRIN). Can you read from the proceedings of our verdict?

SPOKESMAN FOR THE SANHEDRIN: We find Oedipus not guilty of the murder of his father because he acted in self-defense. We find Oedipus not guilty of incest because he did not know that the woman he married and impregnated was his mother. Therefore, we judge that Oedipus lacked mental state of specific intent which is required for the offense of incest. Oedipus did not know who his natural father and mother were.

NASI: Can you read our reasoning behind this verdict?

SPOKESMAN FOR THE SANHEDRIN: First, the Oracle (the *Pythia*) tells Laius that his son Oedipus, upon becoming a man, will kill Laius and marry his wife (Oedipus's mother).

NASI: Go on.

SPOKESMAN FOR THE SANHEDRIN: Second, Laius attempts to kill his son.

NASI: Yes?

SPOKESMAN FOR THE SANHEDRIN: Third, as a direct result of Laius' attempts to kill his son, Oedipus is rescued and adopted by King Polybus and Queen Merope of Corinth.

NASI: And?

SPOKESMAN FOR THE SANHEDRIN: Fourth, Oedipus grows up thinking Polybus is his father and Merope his mother.

NASI: Continue.

SPOKESMAN FOR THE SANHEDRIN: Fifth, Oedipus overhears a man questioning his identity.

NASI: What does Oedipus do?

SPOKESMAN FOR THE SANHEDRIN: Sixth, confused, Oedipus journeys to the Oracle to seek information about the identity of his natural parents.

NASI: What does he learn?

SPOKESMAN FOR THE SANHEDRIN: Seventh, the Oracle does not answer this question. Instead, she tells Oedipus that he is fated to kill his father and marry his mother.

NASI: Aha.

SPOKESMAN FOR THE SANHEDRIN: Eighth, Oedipus becomes frightened and flees from Corinth to avoid hurting his supposed parents.

NASI: I can see that.

SPOKESMAN FOR THE SANHEDRIN: Ninth, Oedipus kills an older man in self-defense over a quarrel regarding right-of-way at a crossing on the road to Thebes. Oedipus does not know that man was his biological father. Indeed, he thinks King Polybus of Corinth is his biological father.

NASI: And?

SPOKESMAN FOR THE SANHEDRIN: Tenth, Oedipus solves the riddle of the Sphinx which has been terrorizing Thebes. But despite the fact that Oedipus is highly intelligent, he remained trapped by Greek fatalism.

NASI: Go on.

SPOKESMAN FOR THE SANHEDRIN: Eleventh, in response to this, Oedipus is rewarded with the Kingship of Thebes and is wed to Queen Jocasta, the widow of King Laius. There is not the slightest shred of evidence that Oedipus had any sense that Jocasta was his mother. Indeed, he thought that the Dorian Merope, the wife of King Polybus, was his mother.

NASI: Did you then find Oedipus not guilty of any crime?

SPOKESMAN FOR THE SANHEDRIN: Only one act, esteemed sir, an act of which he has not been accused.

NASI: If he has not been accused, this court cannot find Oedipus guilty, and no punishment can be assessed.

SPOKESMAN FOR THE SANHEDRIN: We understand this, *Adoni.* Yet this act is so destructive, we must comment on it.

VICE-PRESIDENT OF THE SANHEDRIN: And what is this act?

SPOKESMAN FOR THE SANHEDRIN: Oedipus taking out his own eyes. The prohibition against self-injury occurs in our Holy Torah. "Ye are the children of the Lord your God. You shall not cut yourself nor make any baldness between your eyes for the dead."[1]

NASI: Thank you. (turning to NATHAN), So you are saying that Oedipus did not accept his acquittal?

NATHAN: He did not, Adoni, He insisted that he was guilty.

NASI: How do you know this?

NATHAN: He shouted: "I am guilty! I am guilty! I am guilty of patricide and incest. I am a pollutant, the worst of the worst."

NASI: So, what has changed? Why have you come back?

NATHAN: Oedipus is able to accept his acquittal now.

NASI (to OEDIPUS): Is this true, Oedipus?

---

1. Deuteronomy 14:1

OEDIPUS (haltingly). Yes.

NASI: Can you tell me what has changed for you?

OEDIPUS: My daughter reminded me of what I said when I first entered Colonus after being banished from Thebes.

NASI: What had you said, my good man?

OEDIPUS (turning to ISMENE): You wrote down what I said, dear daughter?

ISMENE: I did, father.

NASI: What were his exact words, my dear woman?

ISMENE: (looking at the same piece of parchment she had before): "And yet in nature how was I evil? I who was but requiting a wrong, so that, had I been acting with knowledge, even then I could not be accounted wicked; but, as it was, all unknowing went I-whither I went—while they who wronged me knowingly sought my ruin."[2]

NASI: Thank you, my dear dear woman. (to OEDIPUS) You see, my noble man, you agreed all along with our verdict.

OEDIPUS: But then, I took out my eyes out needlessly.

SPOKESMAN FOR THE SANHEDRIN (to the NASI): We did comment on that act, which he had not been accused of.

NASI: Can you refresh my memory?

SPOKESMAN FOR THE SANHEDRIN: Oedipus' taking out his eyes. The prohibition against self-injury occurs in our Holy Torah. "Ye are the children of the Lord your God. You shall

---

2. Sophocles, *Oedipus at Colonus*, lines 274–277.

not cut yourself nor make any baldness between your eyes for the dead."[3]

NASI: Yes, I remember. It was a needless self-destructive act.

OEDIPUS (moaning): I ruined my life.

NASI: My dear man, we bemoan the act, we do not condemn you. Your life is not ruined.

OEDIPUS: How can you say this? I cannot *see* what you are saying.

NASI: But can you *hear* what I am saying?

OEDIPUS: What do you mean?

NASI: Sometimes, we can be betrayed by our eyes.

OEDIPUS: I still do not understand.

NATHAN (to OEDIPUS): Do you remember the story of Samson we told you?

OEDIPUS: I am not certain.

NATHAN: How he was betrayed by his eyes.

OEDIPUS: How again?

NATHAN: His 'following his eyes" led to his betraying the source of his strength to the Philistines

SOPHOCLES (to OEDIPUS) : Do you remember what Teiresias said?

OEDIPUS: I am not sure.

---

3. Deuteronomy 14:1

SOPHOCLES: He said: "Sometimes we are blinded by our eyes."[4]

ISMENE: Do you remember what you said when you first entered Colonus?

OEDIPUS: What did I say?

ISMENE: You said , "Behold the man whom you seek! For in sound is my sight, as the saying hath it."[5]

NATHAN: Insight can be more important than sight, my dear Oedipus.

SOPHOCLES: There is seeing and then there is *seeing*.

NASI: Do you think you can accept your blindness, my dear Oedipus, and accept your acquittal?

ISMENE: Can you, father? I love you very much.

OEDIPUS (crying): I will try.

Scene I-2. Oedipus and Ismene leave the Sanhedrin
together, accompanied by Nathan and Sophocles.

NATHAN: Well, my dear friend, Oedipus, finally you can start anew.

OEDIPUS: What do you mean?

SOPHOCLES: You have finally accepted your acquittal.

OEDIPUS: I said I would try.

ISMENE (sharply): Father, you said you would.

---

4. Sophocles, *Oedipus the King*, lines 413–415.
5. Sophocles, *Oedipus at Colonus*, lines 138–39.

OEDIPUS: My daughter, I said I would try.

ISMENE (visibly distressed): You said you would, father.

OEDIPUS: Look at me, I am old and blind. What good am I?

ISMENE (putting her arms around OEDIPUS): What good are you? You are my father. I need you. I will help you.

NATHAN (to ISMENE): I think your father needs to digest all that has happened.

SOPHOCLES (to OEDIPUS): Don't try to deal with all this now. You have been through a most difficult ordeal.

NATHAN (to OEDIPUS): Yes, you must rest and in several days, we will begin to speak about the future.

ISMENE (more composed): Yes, father, you must rest now, and things will become clearer in a few days.

Scene I-3. Nathan and Sophocles meet with Ismene in her room the next week to discuss the situation.

ISMENE: I think my father feels a little lost right now.

SOPHOCLES: Yes, I agree. He has come a long way in agreeing to try to accept emotionally his acquittal.

ISMENE: But what comes next for him and me? Where do we go? What do we do?

SOPHOCLES: Perhaps the two of you should stay in Judea.

ISMENE: But we don't know the language or the customs. We will feel so isolated here.

NATHAN: If I might suggest, why don't the two of you return to Thebes?

ISMENE: But Thebes is the scene of all the bad that befell him.

NATHAN: That is precisely why you must go back there.

ISMENE: But King Creon will kill him.

SOPHOCLES: My dear Ismene, Creon died during the time your father has been in Judea.

ISMENE: So, who is king now?

SOPHOCLES: There is no king right now, but a group of citizens who administer the city.

ISMENE: So, what would my father do in Thebes?

NATHAN: Perhaps he could begin to teach young people the lessons he has learned here in Jerusalem.

SOPHOCLES: That is a very interesting idea.

ISMENE: What lessons would these be?

NATHAN: I can think of a few important lessons.

ISMENE: But what would they be?

NATHAN: He could teach some of the reasons the Sanhedrin gave in acquitting him.

ISMENE: Which are?

NATHAN: That in the biblical tradition, the father is not afraid that his son will surpass him, that is, go beyond him.

ISMENE: And?

SOPHOCLES: That much of what people call fate is actually entrapment.

NATHAN: That people are entrapped by riddles.

ISMENE: Is there more?

NATHAN: That *insight* may be more important than *physical sight*.

SOPHOCLES: And that *hearing* or perhaps *listening* can substitute for *seeing*.

NATHAN: And that people have free will.

ISMENE: These are all very important lessons. Do you think my father could teach this to students in Thebes?

SOPHOCLES: He could if you would help him? Would you be willing to help him?

ISMENE: Yes, of course, but how would I do this?

NATHAN: You will learn how to do this. We will help you.

SOPHOCLES: Are you willing to try?

ISMENE: Yes, of course.

SOPHOCLES: Let us broach the subject with your father now that he has had some time to rest.

Scene I-4. Nathan and Sophocles meet with Oedipus in his room the next day to raise the issues brought up in their previous conversation with Ismene.

NATHAN: Are you feeling more rested, my dear Oedipus?

OEDIPUS: Yes, I am.

SOPHOCLES: Have you thought of the future?

OEDIPUS: What do you mean?

SOPHOCLES: What you will do? Where you will go?

OEDIPUS: I am old and blind. What can I do?

NATHAN: But you are no longer alone. You have Ismene.

OEDIPUS: But I am a burden for her. I am old and blind.

NATHAN: Ismene does not think so. She wants to be with you.

OEDIPUS: But what can I do? Where will I go?

NATHAN: I think we should separate these two questions.

OEDIPUS: What do you mean?

NATHAN: First, let us ask what you want to do,

SOPHOCLES: And then we can address the question of where you will go.

NATHAN (to OEDIPUS): My dear man, what do you want to do with yourself?

OEDIPUS: What can I do? I am old and blind.

NATHAN: Never mind. Have you learned anything here? Has your experience in Judea changed you in any way?

OEDIPUS (thinking): I don't know. I suppose it has in some ways.

NATHAN: In what ways, Oedipus?

OEDIPUS: I suppose it has changed my thinking in some ways, my approach to life.

NATHAN (pressing Oedipus further): In which ways, Oedipus?

OEDIPUS (haltingly): I suppose I have changed my mind about my being guilty of intentionally killing my father and marrying my mother.

NATHAN: How?

OEDIPUS: I realize now that I was trying to avoid killing my father and marrying my mother.

NATHAN: So how is it you committed those very acts?

OEDIPUS: Because I was misled, indeed entrapped, by the Oracle of Delphi (the Pythia).

NATHAN: How?

OEDIPUS: I asked her who my mother was and who my father was?

NATHAN: Why did you do this?

OEDIPUS: Because a drunken man at a dinner party in Corinth suggested that King Polybus and Queen Meirope were not my natural parents.

NATHAN: Did you believe he was telling you the truth?

OEDIPUS: I did not think so, but I wanted to be certain. This is why I went to see the Oracle of Delphi.

NATHAN: And this is why you asked her the question of who your mother and father were?

OEDIPUS: Yes.

NATHAN: And what did the Oracle answer?

OEDIPUS: That I was going to kill my father and marry my mother.

NATHAN: And what did you do?

OEDIPUS: I ran away from Corinth to try to avoid her prophecy. I did not want to kill my father and marry my mother.

NATHAN: And you thought your father and mother were king and queen of Corinth.

OEDIPUS: Of course.

NATHAN: And do you think others might benefit from learning of your experiences and the reasons for your actions?

OEDIPUS: Yes, I was done in by riddles, and I can teach how destructive riddles can be. They can entrap a person into doing the very thing he is trying to avoid.

SOPHOCLES: But is this not fate (*moira*) and necessity (*ananke*)?

OEDIPUS: No!!! It is entrapment. The Pythia was not some passive predictor of the future. Her evasive riddles brought the commission of these terrible acts on my part. But I was not guilty. If only I had been given parables to help me like Nathan gave to his King David.

NATHAN: So, do you think you could teach this lesson to others? To the young?

OEDIPUS: Yes, with Ismene's help.

NATHAN: So, my friend, you now have a task to immerse yourself in.

OEDIPUS: But where will I do this?

SOPHOCLES: This takes us to the second question.

OEDIPUS: Which is?

SOPHOCLES: Where you will live?

NATHAN: Where do you want to live, Oedipus?

OEDIPUS: I don't know.

NATHAN: Do you want to stay in Jerusalem, or somewhere in Judea?

OEDIPUS: No, I don't know the language here. Besides, people here already know what I have to teach.

NATHAN: So where do you want to go?

OEIDIPUS: I am Greek. I miss Greece.

SOPHOCLES: So, do you want to go back to Corinth?

OEDIPUS: No, I fled there long ago.

SOPHOCLES: Do you want to go back to Colonus?

OEDIPUS: No. I fled there also.

SOPHOCLES: So where do you want to go?

OEDIPUS: To Thebes where I was king. I want to clear my name and to teach the people of Thebes what I have learned here. But I am afraid Creon will kill me.

SOPHOCLES: My dear man, Creon is dead.

OEDIPUS: I did not know this. I shed no tears for him. Who governs the city?

SOPHOCLES: A council of citizens.

OEDIPUS: Do you think they will be open to my returning?.

SOPHOCLES; Yes, they were quite relieved upon the death of Creon. He became a very disliked dictator.

OEDIPUS: Would I be alone?

SOPHOCLES: No, Ismene will go with you.

NATHAN: And Sophocles and I will come also to help get you situated.

OEDIPUS: I am afraid.

SOPHOCLES: That is normal. Rest.

NATHAN: We will talk with Ismene tomorrow and begin to make arrangements.

SOPHOCLES: And in two days, we will send Ismene to you.

NATHAN: In the meantime, Sophocles, can you and I meet?

SOPHOCLES: Of course.

*Scene I-5. Nathan and Sophocles meet alone
at a café later that same day.*

NATHAN: I think we need to develop a plan whereby Oedipus can begin to teach what he has learned in Judea to students in Greece.

SOPHOCLES: I agree.

NATHAN: How can we bring this about?

SOPHOCLES: I have a friend, Theodectes, the playwright whose son Kallias can help us find students for Oedipus in Thebes.

NATHAN: This is very good but how will he translate his experiences in Judea into a form that students in Thebes will understand?

SOPHOCLES: This is not an easy question.

NATHAN: Do you know something, Sophocles? I think I need to better understand the journey of Oedipus in leaving his adopted home in Corinth and returning to Thebes.

SOPHOCLES: How will you do this?

NATHAN: I think I need to experience what happened to Oedipus more personally. I'll tell you what. I will travel to Corinth on my own to try to investigate separately what happened to Oedipus there.

SOPHOCLES: Yes, you can look at it with fresh eyes.

NATHAN: Will you meet me in Corinth and travel with me to Delphi?

SOPHOCLES: Why?

NATHAN: I want to experience what happened there to Oedipus. I want to retrace his steps.

SOPHOCLES: Fair enough.

NATHAN: And then we can travel to Thebes together.

SOPHOCLES: This is an excellent idea. We will retrace part of Oedipus's journey from Corinth to Thebes

NATHAN: And when we arrive in Thebes, we will build on this experience to formulate a plan to help Oedipus develop a teaching program.

SOPHOCLES: First we must meet with Ismene.

*Scene I-6. Nathan and Sophocles meet with
Ismene in her room the next day.*

SOPHOCLES: Thank you for meeting with us, Ismene. We
wanted to talk to you about making arrangements for your
journey back to the harbor in Piraeus.

NATHAN: And also your father's mood.

ISMENE: Of course. He is frightened, I am sure, but he does
know I will be with him, does he not?

NATHAN: Yes, of course, but it is a big change for him, even if it
is a change he wants, and he is naturally frightened.

ISMENE: All changes are frightening; even those we want.

NATHAN: Maybe especially those we want.

SOPHOCLES: I have arranged for a student in Thebes, Kallias, to
help you and your father develop your program to teach the
young.

ISMENE: Who is this Kallias?

SOPHOCLES: Kallias comes from a respected family in Thebes.
He is the son of Theodectes the playwright, an old friend of
mine.

NATHAN: This should help your father's adjustment back to Thebes and ease any fears he might have that he is in any danger.

ISMENE: This is very good. Where and when will we meet this
Kallias?

SOPHOCLES: When we disembark in Piraeus.

ISMENE: Will we all be travelling together from Jaffa?

NATHAN: No, I need a little longer to get ready. I will meet you in Thebes

ISMENE (to SOPHOCLES): Will you be travelling with us to Thebes?

SOPHOCLES: No, I will travel with you and your father to Piraeus, but then leave you to meet Nathan who is travelling to Greece separately. Kallias will bring your father and you from Piraeus to Thebes.

ISMENE: When do we begin our journey back to Thebes?

SOPHOCLES: Your father and you and I will travel from Jerusalem in a week to Jaffa and from there we will board a ship to Piraeus, where I will leave you in Kallias's hands. As I said before, Nathan is travelling separately, and I will meet him in Corinth and from there we will go to Delphi and then to Thebes.

Scene I-7. Two days later, Ismene comes to visit her father Oedipus in his room. She takes him by the hand to walk around Jerusalem one last time.

ISMENE (comes into Oedipus's room and throws her arms around him): Father.

OEDIPUS (weeping): Is this you, my daughter?

ISMENE: Yes, father. It is me. How are you?

OEDIPUS: I don't know.

ISMENE: Are you excited to be returning to Thebes?

OEDIPUS: I am frightened.

ISMENE: Are you not also excited?

OEDIPUS: I am frightened.

ISMENE: Why, father?

OEDIPUS: What will I do?

ISMENE: You will teach. We have discussed this.

OEDIPUS: What will I teach, daughter?

ISMENE: You will teach what you have learned in Jerusalem, in Judea.

OEDIPUS: But will they listen to me?

ISMENE: They will, father, I will help you.

OEDIPUS: But you have been in exile from Thebes as well.

ISMENE: But Creon is dead now, father, and Thebes is now governed by a council of citizens.

OEDIPUS: But do you know anyone in this council? How do you know we will be welcomed?

ISMENE: Dear father, Sophocles has arranged for us to be met in Piraeus by a young man named Kallias, who comes from a prominent family in Thebes today. He will help us adjust. Now, let us walk around the city of Jerusalem one last time. We leave for Jaffa tomorrow.

Scene I-8. Two weeks later, Oedipus, Ismene and Sophocles board a ship in Jaffa and travel to the Greek port in Piraeus, Nathan has already traveled separately by himself to Corinth.

SOPHOCLES (to OEDIPUS): My dear man, how do you feel about returning to Thebes after all this time?

OEDIPUS: Apprehensive, and a bit frightened.

SOPHOCLES: That is to be expected. You have been away a long time. (to ISMENE) How do you feel, Ismene?

ISMENE: I feel excited.

SOPHOCLES: But not frightened?

ISMENE: No, curious and expectant, but not frightened.

SOPHOCLES: What are you curious about?

ISMENE: How all this will work out.

SOPHOCLES: What do you mean? Are you curious about what Oedipus will teach, with your assistance?

ISMENE: No, not really. I think he will teach the lessons that he learned in Judea.

SOPHOCLES: And what are these?

ISMENE: I think he will teach two important lessons.

SOPHOCLES: Which are?

ISMENE: That the Greek idea of fate is nothing but entrapment brought about by riddles.

SOPHOCLES: You said there are two lessons. What is the other?

ISMENE: That *seeing* can be limiting. *Hearing*, specifically *listening*, can bring insight that *seeing* alone cannot.

SOPHOCLES: Are there any others?

ISMENE: I think we will start with these.

SOPHOCLES (to OEDIPUS): Do you agree with this?

OEDIPUS: Yes, but I am still apprehensive.

SOPHOCLES: Why are you still apprehensive?.

OEDIPUS: For two reasons.

SOPHOCLES: What are these two reasons?

OEDIPUS: First, to whom will I teach these lessons? Who will be my students? How will I find them?

SOPHOCLES: And secondly?

OEDIPUS: How will I teach these lessons? What method will I use?

SOPHOCLES (to ISMENE): Do you have these concerns as well?

ISMENE: To some degree, yes, I do.

SOPHOCLES: Let me deal with the first issue first-how you will find students.

ISMENE: Go on, please.

SOPHOCLES: I have arranged for Kallias to meet you when you land at Piraeus.

ISMENE: You have mentioned Kallias before. But who is he? Can you tell us more about him?

SOPHOCLES: As I mentioned before, he is the son of an old friend of mine, Theodectes, and comes from a respected family in Thebes. He is a very sensitive and open young man.

OEDIPUS: But how will he help me get students?

SOPHOCLES: He has taught students himself and is very well respected.

OEDIPUS: Do you know him?

SOPHOCLES: Yes, and I know his whole family. His father is a playwright and his brother has acted in several of my plays.

ISMENE: This is very good. Where and when will we meet this Kallias?

SOPHOCLES: As I said before, when we disembark in Piraeus. And he will bring you back to Thebes.

OEDIPUS: Will you not come with us?

SOPHOCLES: No, as I said to Ismene several days ago, I will leave you to meet Nathan who is travelling to Greece separately. Kallias will bring your father and you from Piraeus to Thebes. And Nathan and I will meet you in Thebes within the month.

OEDIPUS: But will we be safe without you?

SOPHOCLES: Yes, and it is important that you have time to adjust without me. Kallias will take good care of both of you.

ISMENE: And what will you and Nathan be doing?

SOPHOCLES: We will be working on the second question you raise. Finding a good method for you to teach the young Thebans the lessons your father and you have learned in Judea.

Scene I-9. Oedipus, Ismene and Sophocles disembark in Piraeus where they are met by Kallias. Sophocles goes on to meet Nathan in Corinth. Oedipus, Ismene and Kallias will travel to Thebes.

SOPHOCLES: Here we are back in Greece.

OEDIPUS: Where are we?

SOPHOCLES: In Piraeus.

ISMENE: Where is the man we are supposed to meet?

SOPHOCLES: The man is Kallias. Please stay with your father while I try to find him.

ISMENE: All right. Will you be gone long?

SOPHOCLES: I should not think so. Please stay with your father.

ISMENE (to OEDIPUS): Can I get you something to drink, father?

OEDIPUS: Yes, but don't leave me. I don't know where I am.

ISMENE: I won't leave you, father. (*She leaves and comes back with a drink*). Here is a drink, father.

OEDIPUS: Thank you, my daughter.

ISMENE: I see Sophocles coming back with a young man, father.

SOPHOCLES (returning): My friends, let me introduce you to Kallias, the man I told you about.

KALLIAS (to OEDIPUS AND ISMENE): It is my honor to meet both of you. Sophocles has told me much about both of you.

ISMENE: We are honored to meet you as well, sir.

KALLIAS: Thank you.

OEDIPUS: You will stay with us, won't you? Sophocles has told us he is leaving us here with you. You will take us to Thebes?

KALLIAS: I will stay with you. There is no need for you to worry. I will accompany you to Thebes.

SOPHOCLES (to OEDIPUS and ISMENE): I will leave you in good hands now, and Nathan and I will meet you again in Thebes.

(Sophocles exits the scene).

KALLIAS (to OEDIPUS and ISMENE) : I have found an inn where you can rest overnight.

OEDIPUS (anxiously and suspiciously): Will you be staying with us?

KALLIAS (reassuringly): Yes. And I have arranged a coach to begin our journey to Thebes tomorrow. Now let us go to the inn so you can rest from your journey here from Judea.

Scene I-10. Oedipus and Ismene board a coach with Kallias and begin their journey to Thebes.

KALLIAS (to both OEDIPUS AND ISMENE): Are the two of you comfortable?

OEDIPUS (nervously): I don't know where I am, or where we are going?

ISMENE: Father, we are going with Kallias to Thebes in a coach.

OEDIPUS: And who exactly are you again, Kallias?

KALLIAS: I am the son of Theodectes, a friend of Sophocles.

OEDIPUS: And again, Why have you come to us?

KALLIAS: Sophocles has asked me to help you settle in Thebes and also to help you find students.

ISMENE: How will you do this, Kallias?

KALLIAS: I have studied myself in the Lyceum in Athens. I know how young people in Greece think. They are a bit lost.

ISMENE: How, Kallias?

KALLIAS: They believe very much that things are fated, That they are destined to do what they will do and there is no way to change their fate.

ISMENE: Yes, that is how I was raised as well.

KALLIAS: Thinking this way can be very paralyzing and young people in Thebes are looking for a different way of approaching their lives.

ISMENE: Yes, I understand this.

OEDIPUS: And how can I help young people change this view?

KALLIAS: You can tell young people in Thebes about your life and how your experience in Judea has changed your thinking.

ISMENE: Can you find my father some students who will listen to him?

KALLIAS: Yes, I am certain I can. My father Theodectes is very well known in Thebes. He is a playwright.

OEDIPUS: Do you think these students will listen to me?

KALLIAS: Yes, if we help you present the material in the right way.

OEDIPUS: I am very tired; I need to close my eyes.

ISMENE: Try to sleep, father. We don't need to answer all these questions now.

KALLIAS: Yes, rest.

Oedipus falls asleep. Ismene and Kallias continue to talk.

ISMENE: And what is this "right way," Kallias?

KALLIAS: This is what Sophocles and Nathan are meeting about. They will come up with a teaching plan, and I will supply the students.

ISMENE: And what will I do, Kallias?

KALLIAS: You will be an intermediary between your father and me, and also help him feel more comfortable in Thebes.

ISMENE: Do you think I have anything to offer?

KALLIAS: I think you have a great deal to offer, Ismene.

*Scene I-11. Sophocles meets Nathan
at an inn in Corinth.*

SOPHOCLES: Did you have an easy journey here?

NATHAN: The sea was a bit turbulent, but it was generally all right.

SOPHOCLES: So, what have you discovered here? What have you learned?

NATHAN: I met and talked to a number of people who remembered Oedipus when he was growing up in the palace of King Polybus and Queen Merope.

SOPHOCLES: And what have you learned?

NATHAN: It isn't so much what I have learned factually, but more about how people saw young Oedipus as he was growing up here.

SOPHOCLES: This is most interesting. How did people see young Oedipus?

NATHAN: Well, of course, different people didn't see him in just one way, but I was able to discern a general impression that people had of Oedipus as he was growing up in Corinth..

SOPHOCLES: And what did they tell you their impression was?

NATHAN: They uniformly liked him. Some people I talked to did not know him as well as others I talked to, of course.

SOPHOCLES: And how did they describe him?

NATHAN: As serious. Honest and sincere.

SOPHOCLES: Anything else?

NATHAN: That although he was generally a very gentle personality, he would occasionally become very angry when he felt an injustice was being done. Was that your view of him when you knew him in Thebes?

SOPHOCLES: Yes, it was. He would take things very much to heart. When Thebes was struck by the pestilence, Oedipus took it very much to heart, as if he was somehow personally responsible for it, which of course he was later told he was.

NATHAN: Some inner sense?

SOPHOCLES: Perhaps.

NATHAN: But people felt he was somewhat the same way when he was growing up in Corinth.

SOPHOCLES: What do you mean?

NATHAN: That he seemed to feel personally responsible if anything went awry in Corinth.

SOPHOCLES: Did people you talked to think that Oedipus was a happy person?

NATHAN: They reported he was a quiet person who generally seemed content but would take things to heart if something went wrong around him.

SOPHOCLES: Did people describe his relationship with King Polybus and Queen Merope?

NATHAN: Only when I asked them specifically.

SOPHOCLES: What did they answer?

NATHAN: People said he was very close with his parents.

SOPHOCLES: Did Polybus and Merope have any other children?

NATHAN: It seems not.

SOPHOCLES: Did Oedipus have many friends outside his family?

NATHAN: Some, but not many.

SOPHOCLES: But Oedipus suddenly left Corinth at a certain point. Did anyone you talked to comment on this?

NATHAN: Yes, everyone I talked to commented on this.

SOPHOCLES: What did people say?

NATHAN: That he was very family-oriented.

SOPHOCLES: Is this all they said?

NATHAN: No, everyone agreed that suddenly Oedipus changed.

SOPHOCLES: How?

NATHAN: He had become nervous and restless.

SOPHOCLES: Did people know why?

NATHAN: They did not seem to be certain.

SOPHOCLES: How did this manifest itself?

NATHAN: Oedipus suddenly started spending much time alone.

SOPHOCES: Was this all?

NATHAN: No, people reported that Oedipus began to lose his patience easily and behave erratically.

SOPHOCLES: And?

NATHAN: Then he suddenly left.

SOPHOCLES: Where did he go?

NATHAN: People were not sure. Some people said Oedipus went to Thebes, others said he went to Delphi.

SOPHOCLES: Where did most people think he went?

NATHAN: To Delphi.

SOPHOCLES: Well, we both have thought Oedipus went to Delphi. Did he come back to Corinth?

NATHAN: Yes, people I talked to said he did come back but in a very agitated mood.

SOPHOCLES: Did he stay in Corinth for a while?

NATHAN: No, people said that Oedipus packed his belongings and immediately left Corinth.

SOPHOCLES: Did they know where he was going?

NATHAN: No, but some people reported that they had later heard he solved the riddle of the Sphinx, a creature that was terrifying Thebes.

SOPHOCLES: Did they hear of him again?

NATHAN: Some did.

SOPHOCLES: What did they hear?

NATHAN: That the King of Thebes had been killed and that Oedipus had married the widowed queen and became king himself.

SOPHOCLES: Did he have any contact with King Polybus and Queen Meirope?

NATHAN; No, people reported Oedipus simply never set foot in Corinth again.

SOPHOCLES: Did people know how King Polybus and Queen Meirope felt about this?

NATHAN: People reported that they were shocked and tried to reach out to Oedipus.

SOPHOCLES: Did he respond?

NATHAN: No, not that anyone remembers.

SOPHOCLES: So, is this the last they heard of Oedipus?

NATHAN: No, they reported that when King Polybus had died, a messenger was sent to Thebes to inform Oedipus that he was now King of Corinth.

SOPHOCLES: And then?

NATHAN: They heard that Oedipus had been exiled from Thebes, and then nothing more.

SOPHOCLES: This is all very interesting but how is this going to help us formulate a teaching program for Oedipus back in Thebes? Where do we go from here?

NATHAN: I think we should go to Delphi and try to understand what Oedipus learned there that so shook him.

SOPHOCLES: I agree. Let us leave tomorrow, retracing Oedipus's journey from Corinth to Delphi.

Scene I-12. Sophocles and Nathan arrive in Delphi.
They sit at a cafe.

SOPHOCLES: Well, Nathan, here we are in Delphi.

NATHAN: Can you tell me something about Delphi and why it is so important in your tradition?

SOPHOCLES: Delphi is the seat of our most important Greek temple and oracle of Apollo. It lies on the steep lower slope of Mount Parnassus where our gods reside. We are ten kilometers (six miles) from the Gulf of Corinth.

NATHAN: Can you tell me something about the history of Delphi?

SOPHOCLES: We consider Delphi to be the center of the world. Our god Zeus released two eagles, one from the east, the other from the west, and caused them to fly toward the center. They met in Delphi, and the spot is marked by a stone called the *omphalos*.

NATHAN: What does *omphalos* mean?

SOPHOCLES: *Omphalos* means "navel".

NATHAN: Is there anything else I need to know about the omphalos?

SOPHOCLES: We believe that the oracle at Delphi originally belonged to Gaea, the Earth goddess, and was guarded by her child Python, the serpent.

NATHAN: What do you mean: "originally?" Do you not believe the oracle still belongs to this Gaea?

SOPHOCLES: No, the infant god Apollo was said to have slain the serpent Python and founded his own oracle there.

NATHAN: So, Greeks now believe the oracle is that of Apollo?

SOPHOCLES: Yes. But it is a bit more complicated.

NATHAN: More complicated?

SOPHOCLES: Yes.

NATHAN: How, more complicated?

SOPHOCLES: When Apollo's arrows pierced the serpent, its body fell into a fissure and great fumes arose from the crevice as its carcass rotted. All those who stood over the gaping fissure fell into sudden, often violent, trances. In this state, it was believed that Apollo would possess the person and fill him with divine presence.

NATHAN: *Baruch ha Shem* (God be praised), you Greeks have such strange customs.

SOPHOCLES: Well, this is what we have been taught since childhood.

NATHAN: Is this oracle a man or a woman?

SOPHOCLES: As you know from the trial of Oedipus in the Sanhedrin, the oracle is a woman. She is called the Pythia.

NATHAN: And tell me again, my dear friend, how does this Pythia transmit information?

SOPHOCLES: As you know from the trial of Oedipus in the Sanhedrin in Jerusalem, the Pythia is asked questions and answers them. Do you remember?

NATHAN: Of course I interrogated the Pythia as a witness. She was an older woman. But was the Pythia always old?

SOPHOCLES: Not originally. At first the Pythia was a young woman, a pure, chaste beautiful young virgin.

NATHAN: Why was there this change ? Was it because the older woman was assumed to be wiser than a younger woman?

SOPHOCLES: Not exactly. There was another reason.

NATHAN: What was this other reason?

SOPHOCLES: Well, beautiful young virgins were prone to attracting negative attention from the men who sought their council, which resulted in oracles being raped and violated.

NATHAN: So, what happened?

SOPHOCLES: Older women of at least 50 years old began to fill the position, and as a reminder of what used to be, they would dress in the virginal garments of old.

NATHAN: I think I understand. What is the exact method by which the Pythia is asked questions and answers them? How would the process work exactly?

SOPHOCLES: First the Pythia purifies herself by fasting, drinking holy water and bathing in the sacred Castalian Spring.

NATHAN: You say "first", what happens next ?

SOPHOCLES: The Pythia would assume her position upon a tripod seat, clasping laurel reeds in one hand and a dish of spring water in the other. Positioned above the gaping fissure, the vapors of the ancient vanquished serpent would wash over her, and she would enter the realm of the divine.

NATHAN: I can see this process is not so simple. Could anyone come to ask the Pythia a question?

SOPHOCLES: No, of course not. Many people from all over Greece and beyond want to ask the Pythia a question, so the process was much more involved.

NATHAN: So how does it work?

SOPHOCLES: People from all over Greece come to Delphi to ask the oracle a question. We call them "consultants".

NATHAN: Do they see the oracle when they arrive?

SOPHOCLES: No. when these "consultants" arrive in Delphi, they meet with priests who determine which cases are genuine and which not. And moreover, they must decide how to frame their questions.

NATHAN: So, this is the process Oedipus went through when he arrived at Delphi from Corinth?

SOPHOCLES: Undoubtedly.

NATHAN: So, at this point would Oedipus have been able to ask his question?

SOPHOCLES: No, those who are approved then have to undergo a variety of other traditions.

NATHAN: Such as?

SOPHOCLES: Such as carrying laurel wreaths to the temple. It is also encouraged for consultants to provide a monetary donation as well as an animal to be sacrificed.

NATHAN: Why is it important for an animal to be sacrificed?

SOPHOCLES: Once the animal has been sacrificed, its guts are studied. If the signs are seen as unfavorable, the consultant could be sent home.

NATHAN: Without having a chance to ask the Pythia a question?

SOPHOCLES: That is correct. However, if the signs are favorable, the consultant is allowed to approach the Pythia and ask his question.

NATHAN: So, then the Pythia would give her answer?

SOPHOCLES: Sometimes, but at other times, the Pythia would utter incomprehensible words that the priests would translate.

NATHAN: Once the consultant receives his answer, what would happen next?

SOPHOCLES: The consultant would journey home to act upon the advice of the oracle.

NATHAN: Can we assume that this is what happened in the case of Oedipus?

SOPHOCLES: Yes, but remember the answer the Pythia gave you when you interrogated her at the trial of Oedipus in the Sanhedrin.

NATHAN: Yes, she refused to acknowledge that she had not answered the question Oedipus came to ask her.

SOPHOCLES: Yes, after hearing his lineage questioned by a drunken young man at a dinner party, Oedipus went to the Pythia to ask her whether King Polybus and Queen Meirope of Corinth were his natural parents.

NATHAN: And the Pythia did not answer him; not that question at least.

SOPHOCLES: No, she answered him that he was destined to kill his father and marry his mother.

NATHAN: Whom he thought were the King and Queen of Corinth.

SOPHOCLES: So, Oedipus fled Corinth immediately to avoid doing these horrible things.

NATHAN: And in the process wound up bringing about exactly what he was trying to avoid: killing his natural father Laius and marrying his natural mother Jocasta.

SOPHOCLES: Even though he did not know that these people were his natural father and mother.

NATHAN: No, he mistakenly had thought that the King and Queen of Corinth were his biological parents.

SOPHOCLES: And this led to Oedipus killing his natural father and marrying his natural mother.

NATHAN: And it was the withholding and obscuring of information and indeed riddling, not some abstract fate, that led to Oedipus bringing about what he was trying to avoid.

SOPHOCLES: Yes, your brilliant questioning of the Pythia at Oedipus's trial at the Sanhedrin in Jerusalem convinced me of this.

NATHAN: And it is this lesson that must be central to what Oedipus can teach to the young Thebans.

SOPHOCLES: And also the lesson that insight can be deeper than outer sight.

NATHAN: That our story of Samson reveals how a person be undone by his eyes.

SOPHOCLES: And the destructive role of riddles in this process.

NATHAN: As compared to that of parables.

SOPHOCLES: Let us now journey to Thebes and begin to prepare a teaching program for Oedipus where he will be able to transmit this method to young Thebans.

NATHAN: And who knows, perhaps other themes may emerge in Oedipus's teaching program.

SOPHOCLES: Let us resume this conversation in Thebes.

Scene I-13. Sophocles and Nathan arrive in Thebes to plan a teaching program for Oedipus. They meet in a room Sophocles has rented.

SOPHOCLES: So here we are in Thebes.

NATHAN: This is where Oedipus's problems began.

SOPHOCLES: I think they began in Corinth.

NATHAN: But in Thebes before that.

SOPHOCLES: Actually, in Delphi.

NATHAN: Twice.

SOPHOCLES: Twice?

NATHAN: First, before Oedipus was born, when his father Laius was warned by the Pythia that his son would kill him if he reached man's estate.

SOPHOCLES: Yes, and what was the second?

NATHAN: When Oedipus came here from Corinth after he heard a rumor that King Polybus and Queen Meirope of Corinth were not his natural parents.

SOPHOCLES: You are correct. How can we use these events to help Oedipus plan his teaching program here in Thebes?

NATHAN: Let us map out topics for Oedipus.

SOPHOCLES: Where do we start?

NATHAN: First, that what is called "fate" is actually not having the proper information to make freeing decisions.

SOPHOCLES: How would Oedipus teach this?

NATHAN: I think by demonstrating how a student cannot solve a problem without clear information as to what the problem is.

SOPHOCLES: Without that information, teaching can be seen as a riddle, actually decreasing a student's ability to analyze and solve a life situation, indeed distracting him.

NATHAN: Can you think of any riddles in Greek history that illustrate this?

SOPHOCLES: Yes, I can think of several.

NATHAN: Can you tell me one?

SOPHOCLES: Herodotus, our first historian, tells us of Croesus, the king of Lydia, who asked the Pythia if he should attack Persia.[6]

NATHAN: How did the Pythia answer?

SOPHOCLES: She answered Croesus as follows; "If you cross the river, a great empire will be destroyed."

NATHAN: What did Croesus do?

SOPHOCLES: Oedipus can discuss this in his class.

NATHAN: Are there any other examples Oedipus might develop?

SOPHOCLES: Herodotus tells us that as the Persian Emperor Xerxes marched toward Athens, the citizens debated the meaning of an oracle's prediction that "wooden walls" would save the city.

NATHAN: Does Oedipus know this story?

SOPHOCLES: I would think so. If not, we can help him?

6. Herodotus, 1961 *Histories,* Translated by Aubrey de Selincourt, Baltimore, MD.: Penguin Books.

NATHAN: Why do both of these incidents involve riddles?

SOPHOCLES: I think that in the Greek tradition, a riddle is preferable to plain information.

NATHAN: Why?

SOPHOCLES: Because the Greeks think any fool could understand plain information, but that riddles represent divine speech. which it takes wisdom to discern. [7]

NATHAN: Do you think so?

SOPHOCLES: I used to.

NATHAN: And now.

SOPHOCLES: I am not so sure.

NATHAN: Are there any other riddles that you think Oedipus can teach?

SOPHOCLES: Yes, the riddle we call Zeno's paradox.

NATHAN: Is this Zeno the Stoic?

SOPHOCLES: No, this is Zeno of Elea.

NATHAN: What is Zeno's paradox?

SOPHOCLES: It goes like this. A tortoise challenged our famous warrior Achilles to a race, claiming that he would win as long as Achilles gave him a small head start. [8]

---

7. Sophocles, Fragment 771.

8. Smith, B. Sidney (10 Apr 2014). Zeno's Paradox of the Tortoise and Achilles. *Platonic Realms Interactive Mathematics Encyclopedia*:http://platonicrealms.com/encyclopedia/Zeno's-Paradox-of-the-Tortoise-and-Achilles, and from *Oxford Classical Dictionary, The* (1970), edited by M. G. L. Hammond and H. H. Scullard.

NATHAN: This doesn't make any sense. Achilles could run much faster than a tortoise could.

SOPHOCLES: This is the paradox

NATHAN: So what happens?

SOPHOCLES: Achilles accepted the tortoise's challenge but asked him how big a start he needed.

NATHAN: What did the tortoise answer?

SOPHOCLES: Ten meters.

NATHAN: Still, Achilles should have won the race.

SOPHOCLES: No, Achilles conceded because of the way in which Zeno constructed his paradox.

NATHAN: Why? How? It makes no sense. It is misleading. Of course, Achilles will catch the tortoise.

SOPHOCLES: You will see.

NATHAN: But this is misleading.

SOPHOCLES: I have come to see much of our education in Greece is misleading in this way.

NATHAN: Can you think of any other examples?

SOPHOCLES: Yes, the riddle of Homer.[9]

NATHAN: What is this riddle?

SOPHOCLES: I am certain Oedipus knows this riddle. What is important is that Homer is so preoccupied in trying to solve

9. The Oxford Classical Dictionary; Certamen Homeri et Hesiodi, p. 224; Landesman, 1965; Mandilaras, 1992.

a children's riddle he is presented with that it distracts him from his surroundings.

NATHAN: Do you think Oedipus can use this in his teaching?

SOPHOCLES: Yes. We can help him develop it.

END OF ACT I

Act II: Oedipus Teaches (and Learns)

Scene II-1. Sophocles and Nathan meet with Oedipus and Ismene in a small storefront in Thebes to discuss their teaching program.

ISMENE: Is this where we will we will hold our classes?

SOPHOCLES: Yes.

NATHAN: It is nothing but a storefront.

SOPHOCLES: This is what schools are like in Greece,

NATHAN: Where will the students sit?

SOPHOCLES: On wooden benches.

NATHAN: Are there no desks?

SOPHOCLES: No.

ISMENE: Where will the teacher sit?

SOPHOCLES: On a chair.

ISMENE: Will I be able to sit on a chair?

SOPHOCLES: I will ask Kallias to see if he can arrange this.

NATHAN: How many students will be in the class?

SOPHOCLES: About ten to twenty boys.

NATHAN: Are there no girls?

SOPHOCLES: No. Only boys are taught in Thebes, and in Greece generally.

NATHAN: How do teachers encourage students to learn in Greece?

SOPHOCLES: They hit their students if they do not learn well enough.

OEDIPUS: I will not allow hitting in this school.

SOPHOCLES: You are the teacher, so you can choose not to allow it.

OEDIPUS: I won't have students afraid to go to my class.

SOPHOCLES: I will ask Kallias to see if he can forbid hitting as a rule of the school.

OEDIPUS: I insist on this.

NATHAN: Let us talk for a little bit on what you will teach.

OEDIPUS: What do you mean?

NATHAN: The exact themes you are trying to teach.

SOPHOCLES: Yes, can we help you list them?

OEDIPUS: What do you think they should be? Can you help me?

NATHAN: I think an overriding theme should be that the Greek concept of fate is actually nothing but withholding of information or presenting it in a misleading manner—often as a riddle.

SOPHOCLES: Like the Pythia's response to you when you asked her the question as to the identity of your parents.

OEDIPUS: Yes, she did not answer my question.

SOPHOCLES: We have found a number of examples of the ambiguous presentation of information in Greek thinking.

ISMENE: What are they?

SOPHOCLES: First, the story of the response of the Pythia to Croesus, the king of Lydia, when he asked her if he should attack Persia?

OEDIPUS: I know this story. It is a good one. Are there any others?

SOPHOCLES: Why don't you use the riddle given to the Athenian leader Themosticles that "wooden walls" would save the city from the Persians.?[10]

OEDIPUS: I only know this story vaguely

SOPHOCLES: Don't worry. We will help you.

ISMENE: Can you think of any other stories?

SOPHOCLES: Yes, the riddle of the death of our great poet Homer.

ISMENE: Do you know this story, father.

OEDIPUS: Yes daughter, I do.

ISMENE: Can you think of any other riddles that my father can tell?

---

10. Herodotus, 1961 *Histories,* Translated by Aubrey de Selincourt,. Baltimore, MD.: Penguin Books.

SOPHOCLES: Yes, Zeno's Paradox.

ISMENE: What is that?

SOPHOCLES: It is the story of a race between Achilles and a tortoise, where Achilles cannot catch the tortoise if the tortoise has a head start.[11]

OEDIPUS: This is a very good story to teach, and I am certain there are many others.

NATHAN: But you have a more personal story to teach as well?

OEDIPUS: What is that?

NATHAN: That insight is more important than sight. And that overreliance on one's eyes can lead a person astray.

SOPHOCLES: Like the biblical story of Samson.

NATHAN: Yes, and also the idea that hearing can be more important than seeing.

OEDIPUS: Do you think I should cover any additional topics?

NATHAN: Let us keep an open mind regarding this and we will see what transpires.

SOPHOCLES: I agree. Have you written down these topics, Ismene?

ISMENE: Yes, of course.

SOPHOCLES: Why don't you and Ismene meet alone with Kallias to plan out the teaching program more specifically?

---

11. Smith, B. Sidney (10 Apr 2014). Zeno's Paradox of the Tortoise and Achilles. *Platonic Realms Interactive Mathematics Encyclopedia*:http://platonicrealms.com/encyclopedia/Zeno's-Paradox-of-the-Tortoise-and-Achilles.

ISMENE (enthusiastically): This is a very good idea.

*Scene II-2. Oedipus and Ismene meet with
Kallias in the same storefront to plan a
teaching program in more detail.*

ISMENE: Thank you for joining us, Kallias.

KALLIAS: Of course, Ismene.

ISMENE: We want to plan out my father's teaching program.

KALLIAS: I am here to help you. Where do we begin?

OEDIPUS: First of all, how many students can we expect in a class?

KALLIAS: Usually classes include from ten to twenty students.

OEDIPUS: How old will they be?

KALLIAS: Typically, from seven to thirteen years of age.

OEDIPUS: Is it possible to get slightly older students?

KALLIAS: What age?

OEDIPUS: Thirteen to sixteen years of age.

KALLIAS: I will try

ISMENE: Will the students be boys or girls or both?

KALLIAS: We only take boys into schools in Greece.

ISMENE: Does that make it right?

KALLIAS: Do you want to change the world?

ISMENE (firmly): Some things need to be changed.

OEDIPUS: Can we get back to discussing what I will teach?

ISMENE: What *we* will teach, father.

OEDIPUS (smiling): What *we* will teach, my daughter?

KALLIAS (somewhat impatiently): What will you jointly teach?

ISMENE: I have made a list.

OEDIPUS (smiling): Thank you, my captain.

KALLIAS: Can you tell me what is on the list?

ISMENE: First, we will teach my father's story of his life.

KALLIAS: Can you be more specific?

ISMENE (resolutely): I have divided the story into different
    stages. Is that all right with you, father?

OEDIPUS: Yes, my daughter. Thank you.

KALLIAS: Can you lay it out for us?

ISMENE: Yes.

KALLIAS: What is the first stage?

ISMENE: My father's life in Corinth as the son of King Polybus
    and Queen Meirope.

KALLIAS (to OEDIPUS): Does this sound right?

OEDIPUS: Yes, I was very content.

KALLIAS (to ISMENE): Please go on.

ISMENE: But then, everything changes. A drunken young man at a dinner party questions my father's identity.

KALLIAS: And?

ISMENE: My father goes to his parents and asks them if what the man says is true.

KALLIAS: And what do they say?

ISMENE: They tell him it is not true and that they are his parents.

KALLIAS (to OEDIPUS): Did you accept that?

OEDIPUS: I wasn't sure. I was bothered.

KALLIAS (somewhat testily): Why?

OEDIPUS: I am not sure.

KALLIAS (to ISMENE): So, what did your father do next?

ISMENE: He went to see the Pythia .

OEDIPUS: I wanted to be certain as to who my parents were.

KALLIAS: So, what happened next?

ISMENE: My father finally was able to see the Pythia.

KALLIAS (to OEDIPUS): What did you ask the Pythia ?

OEDIPUS: Who my parents were. I am feeling anxious.

KALLIAS (to ISMENE): Perhaps you can go on with this. What did the Pythia answer?

ISMENE: That my father would kill his father and marry his mother.

KALLIAS: Whom he thought were the King and Queen of Corinth?

ISMENE: Of course. This is what made my father run away from Corinth and travel to Thebes, and we all know what happened then.

KALLIAS: What?

ISMENE: He mistakenly killed his natural father on the road and then ultimately married the widowed queen who was in fact my father's natural mother.

KALLIAS (somehat impatiently): So, what is the lesson that students can learn from this sad story?

ISMENE: How devastating riddles can be for the people who hear them.

KALLIAS (to ISMENE): I think your father should teach his personal story in a later class. Can he begin by discussing riddles outside of his own life?

OEDIPUS (recovering slightly): Please talk to me directly, Kallias. I will relate the incident of the response of the Pythia to Croesus, the king of Lydia, when he asked her if he should attack Persia?

KALLIAS: Good, will you give any other examples?

OEDIPUS: I don't remember.

ISMENE: You were going to relate the story of the riddle given to the Athenian leader Themosticles that "wooden walls" would save the city from the Persians?[12]

---

12. Herodotus, 1961 *Histories,* Translated by Aubrey de Selincourt,. Baltimore, MD.: Penguin Books.

OEDIPUS: Yes, you were going to help me tell this story.

KALLIAS: Will you tell any other stories?

ISMENE: You are going to teach the story of the misleading lesson of Zeno's Paradox as well.

OEDIPUS: That's right. Thank you for remembering, my dearest daughter.

KALLIAS: Let us move on. Do you have any other lessons you want to teach as well?

ISMENE: Yes, father, you are going to teach the riddle of Homer's death.

OEDIPUS: Yes, I remember.

KALLIAS (somewhat impatiently): Will you be teaching any other stories?

ISMENE (protectively): Yes, father, you want to teach how insight can be more important than sight per se, And that hearing can compensate for seeing.

OEDIPUS: I remember now. And how one can be misled by his eyes.

ISMENE: Yes, father, you will teach the story of Samson, who was undone by "following his eyes."

KALLIAS: These are very good topics. Are there any more topics do you want to cover?

OEDIPUS (haltingly): I am not certain.

KALLIAS: Why don't we see what transpires? We can always add topics. The first problem is to finalize the location of this school and the specific curriculum.

ISMENE: Yes.

KALLIAS (to ISMENE) : Can you and I meet alone tomorrow to discuss the mechanics of how we will recruit students and finalize the use of this storefront and how we may decorate it? Your father does not seem to have the capacity to concentrate on the specific arrangements.

ISMENE: Yes. Where shall we meet?

KALLIAS: At a café down the street. Is this good?

ISMENE: Yes.

Scene II-3. Ismene and Kallias meet alone at a nearby café to discuss the recruitment of students and the mechanics of the course. They begin to discuss their lives.

Ismene enters the café and sits down at a table at which Kallias is already sitting

KALLIAS: Welcome, Ismene. Thank you very much for coming. There was no need to bother your father with this meeting.

ISMENE: No, he needs to rest as much as possible.

KALLIAS: I guess the first thing to talk about is how to recruit students.

ISMENE: Yes.

KALLIAS: I know many people in Thebes. My family is very prominent. My father is Theodectes.

ISMENE: Is he not a very well-known playwright?

KALLIAS: He is, Ismene, and a friend of Sophocles.

ISMENE: You are very fortunate to come from such a distinguished family.

KALLIAS (hesitatingly): Yes, I guess so.

ISMENE: You guess so?

KALLIAS (testily): Let us concentrate at the moment on how we will recruit students.

ISMENE: How will we do this?

KALLIAS: This should be quite easy. My father is part of an elite group of public intellectuals who see their role as advising the council of citizens who have governed Thebes since the death of Creon.

ISMENE (sarcastically): Yes, my dear uncle who loved us so much he wanted us all dead.

KALLIAS (softly): This must have been terrible, my dear Ismene.

ISMENE (wiping away tears): There is no point talking about this now. Let the dead bury the dead. Let us go on with the recruitment plans. How will we go about it?

KALLIAS: I can send an announcement to the citizen's council with an attached letter from my father announcing your father's class. I am certain we will receive responses from more than twenty applicants. Let us say we choose the best twelve applicants to give your father and you a class that is not too small and not too large.

ISMENE: Will you help us in the teaching of the class?

KALLIAS (somewhat resentfully): The center of the class is your father, and of course, you. I am really only an appendage.

ISMENE: No, you are more, Kallias.

KALLIAS: Perhaps. How else can I help you?

ISMENE: We need a building in which to teach the class. Can we use the storefront we met in before?

KALLIAS: Yes, I think we can.

ISMENE: Can we get permission to decorate it?

KALLIAS: Yes, I am sure we can.

ISMENE: Can you get chairs and desks for the students instead of stools?

KALLIAS: This may be more difficult, but I think I will be able to do this.

ISMENE: Can you arrange a class of girls and boys?

KALLIAS: No, that I cannot do, Ismene.

ISMENE: But this is not right.

KALLIAS (somehat irritated): You know only boys go to school in Greece.

ISMENE: Are you upset, Kallias?

KALLIAS: Never mine, Ismene. Tell me more about yourself.

ISMENE: What is there to tell?

KALLIAS: What was your family like?

ISMENE: What do you mean?

KALLIAS: Were your parents happy with each other?

ISMENE: Yes, very happy.

KALLIAS: Were you happy growing up?

ISMENE: Yes, very happy. Until . . .

KALLIAS: Until?

ISMENE: Yes, until.

KALLIAS: Until?

ISMENE: Until a pestilence fell upon Thebes.

KALLIAS: Yes, I remember.

ISMENE: And then everything fell apart.

KALLIAS: Yes, I remember.

ISMENE: What do you remember?

KALLIAS: Your mother hung herself and your father blinded himself.

ISMENE: What else do you remember?

KALLIAS: Your uncle Creon banished your father from Thebes.

ISMENE: And then what?

KALLIAS: Your two brothers killed each other fighting at our *Seventh Gate*.

ISMENE: Do you remember what happened to my sister Antigone?

KALLIAS: I am not sure. What did happen to her?

ISMENE: My *dear* uncle Creon buried my sister alive.

KALLIAS: Why?

ISMENE: Because she defied his order not to bury our slain rebel brother Polyneices.

KALLIAS: Quite a way for a family to disintegrate.

ISMENE (crying): Yes.

KALLIAS: But you escaped.

ISMENE: Perhaps because I was more timid.

KALLIAS: Perhaps to fight another day.

ISMENE: Perhaps.

KALLIAS (somewhat cynically): And now you are reunited with your father who needs you very much.

ISMENE: Yes, and I need him.

KALLIAS (even more cynically): I see he needs you very much.

ISMENE (harshly): You are very fortunate to come from a stable prominent family.

KALLIAS (sadly): Yes, but I have not been happy.

ISMENE (softening): Why have you not been happy?

KALLIAS: It is very difficult to have a father as brilliant, successful and prominent as Theodectes.

ISMENE: Why?

KALLIAS (bitterly): I never quite felt that I could measure up.

ISMENE (softly): Why, you seem like a wonderful man.

KALLIAS: Thank you. I have not always felt that.

ISMENE: Why, Kallias?

KALLIAS: Just because, Ismene, I have always felt inadequate compared to my father.

ISMENE: Why?

KALLIAS: Because I cannot write plays the way he does. Because I am not respected by the community the way he is.

ISMENE: Is that all?

KALLIAS (somewhat roughly): I feel fathers are jealous of their sons. It is common knowledge as to how your father was treated by his father Laius.

ISMENE: Yes, he was put out to die as an infant because Laius had heard a prophecy that my father would kill him when he grew up.

KALLIAS: Do you think your father is jealous of me?

ISMENE: Why would he be jealous, Kallias? Look how you try to help my father and me.

KALLIAS: You don't know older men. Do you like me, Ismene?

ISMENE: Of course I like you, Kallias. But I don't understand why you are upset.

KALLIAS): I like you also, Ismene. But you are not free.

Scene II-4. Oedipus teaches his first class with the help of Ismene and Kallias. He gives examples of often destructive Greek riddles. Sophocles and Nathan are present as well and Nathan provides an example of a parable.

Twelve students sit on chairs with desks before Oedipus who is also sitting on a chair behind a desk. Ismene and Kallias are standing by a board on which they have written an outline. Alec has been chosen to be spokesman for the students. He is thirteen years old.

KALLIAS: Welcome, dear students of Thebes. I want to introduce you to your esteemed teacher, Oedipus, the former King of Thebes and his daughter Ismene.

ALEC (SPOKESMAN FOR THE STUDENTS): Thank you, Kallias. I am Alec and am spokesman for this class. We are honored to be students of Oedipus and Ismene.

OEDIPUS: Dear students, I want to speak to you today of parables and riddles and the damage that riddles can do.

ISMENE: We will start with the lesson we call Zeno's Paradox.

ALEC: What is this "Zeno's Paradox" ?

OEDIPUS: A tortoise challenged our famous warrior Achilles to a race, claiming that he would win as long as Achilles gave him a small head start.

ALEC: This doesn't make any sense. Achilles could run much faster than a tortoise could.

OEDIPUS: Achilles agreed with you. In fact, he laughed at this idea, for of course he was much faster than the slower tortoise.

ALEC: Did Achilles accept the challenge?

OEDIPUS: Yes, of course, but he asked the tortoise how big a start he needed.

ALEC: What did the tortoise answer?

OEDIPUS: Ten meters.

ALEC: How did Achilles respond?

OEDIPUS: He laughed and told the tortoise he would surely lose.

ALEC: So, the tortoise lost the race.

OEDIPUS: No.

ALEC: Why?

OEDIPUS: The tortoise asked Achilles that if he (the tortoise) was given a 10-meter head start, whether Achilles could cover that ground.

ALEC: What did Achilles answer?

OEDIPUS: That he could catch him very quickly.

ALEC: So, the tortoise conceded, and the race was never run?

OEDIPUS: No, actually Achilles conceded.

ALEC: Why? How?

OEDIPUS: The tortoise answered that in that time, he would have gone one meter more. And that in the time Achilles covered that difference, he (the tortoise) would have moved ahead a tenth of a meter.[13]

---

13. Smith, B. Sidney (10 Apr 2014). Zeno's Paradox of the Tortoise and Achilles. *Platonic Realms Interactive Mathematics Encyclopedia*:http://platoni-crealms.com/encyclopedia/Zeno's-Paradox-of-the-Tortoise-and-Achilles.

ISMENE: So according to this way of looking at it, Achilles would never catch the tortoise.

ALEC: This is ridiculous. Of course Achilles would catch the tortoise.

KALLIAS (interjecting): Of course. But the story is told as a riddle which obscures what would be the actual outcome.

ALEC: I see. Do you have any other examples, esteemed Oedipus?

ISMENE: Why don't we turn to the story of King Croesus of Lydia, dearest father?

OEDIPUS: All right, my daughter.

ALEC: Who is this King Croesus, esteemed sir?

OEDIPUS: Probably the world's wealthiest man,

ALEC: What did he do, esteemed teacher?

OEDIPUS: Croesus determined at one point to try to conquer the growing Persian power of Cyrus the Great. He sought the advice of the best of oracles and after careful testing determined that the Pythia would best answer his question.[14]

ALEC: What was his question?

OEDIPUS: Shall I go to war against the Persians?

ALEC: What did the Pythia answer?

OEDIPUS: The Pythia answered: "Go to war and a mighty kingdom will fall."

---

14. Herodotus, 1961 *Histories,* Translated by Aubrey de Selincourt,. Baltimore, MD.: Penguin Book

ALEC: What did Croesus do?

OEDIPUS: He went to war against the Persians,

ALEC: And what happened? Did a great empire fall?

OEDIPUS: It did, but in the opposite way than Croesus interpreted it.

ALEC: How?

OEDIPUS: The great empire that fell was his own.

ALEC: The Persians conquered Lydia?

OEDIPUS: Yes. The Persian King Cyrus crushed his army and conquered Lydia. Only then did Croesus realize that the empire he would destroy was his own.

ALEC: Oh my. I see what you mean. The Pythia misled him. Are there any other examples?

OEDIPUS: Yes, I can think of the riddle presented to the Athenians as the Persian leader Xerxes was marching towards Athens.

ALEC: What was the riddle?

OEDIPUS: I am suddenly weary, Ismene, can you continue?

ISMENE: Yes. I think so. As the Persian leader Xerxes marched toward Athens, the citizens debated the meaning of an oracle's predication that "wooden walls" would save the city.

ALEC: How did they interpret it?

ISMENE (faltering): I am not certain.

KALLIAS (jumping in to rescue Ismene): The Athenian leader Themistocles persuaded the others that this meant the Athenians should fight at sea with their wooden ships.

ALEC: Was he correct?

ISMENE (recovering her thoughts) Yes. The Athenian navy destroyed the Persian fleet as Xerxes looked on in horror. The Spartans sent on to win a great land victory over the Persian fleet as Xerxes looked on horrified.[15]

ALEC: And what was the result?

KALLIAS (smiling triumphantly): The Persian army marched back across a pontoon bridge to Persia.

OEDIPUS (blurting in somewhat resentfully): And they never returned.

ALEC But this is an example of where a riddle was helpful.

ISMENE: But why did the advice have to be in the form of a riddle?

SOPHOCLES (inserting himself into the lesson): Because we Greeks enjoy riddles for their own sake. We think any fool could understand plain information, but riddles represent divine speech which takes intelligence to discern. [16]

ALEC (confused): Do you still enjoy riddles?

SOPHOCLES: I am not so certain. I have come to see that straight talk can be preferable, while riddles can do a lot of damage.

---

15. Herodotus, 1961 *Histories,* Translated by Aubrey de Selincourt, Baltimore, MD.: Penguin Books.

16. Sophockes, Fragment 771.

ALEC: Can you give another example where a riddle can be destructive?

SOPHOCLES: Yes, where it can distract a person from his real life and lead to disaster, and even death.

ALEC: And what is this riddle?

SOPHOCLES: The riddle of Homer. Do you know this riddle, Oedipus?

OEDIPUS: I think so. According to legend, our great blind poet Homer did not know where he was born and he once stopped at Delphi to see if the Oracle could help him. He was told, "The isle of Ios is your mother's country and it shall receive you dead; but beware the riddles of young children."

ALEC: So what happened?

OEDIPUS: As an old man, Homer happened to visit the island of Ios, and when he sat on the shore one day he met some children of local fishermen coming back from the sea and asked them what they had caught. They replied: "What we caught we threw away, and what we didn't catch we kept"

ALEC: What was the answer to this riddle?

OEDIPUS: The answer was "lice". But this was not the lesson of the story.

ALEC: What *was* the lesson of the story?

OEDIPUS: While Homer was trying to figure out the answer to this riddle, he remembered the oracle and realized his time was up. He slipped, bumped his head and died.[17]

---

17. *The Oxford Classical Dictionary*, Certamen Homeri et Hesiodi, p. 224; Landesman, 1965; Mandilaras, 1992.

ALEC: I still don't understand this story. What life lessons can one draw from it?

ISMENE: The meaning we can draw from the story is that one should pay attention to what one is doing and not be distracted.

SOPHOCLES: And this is exactly what riddles do,- they distract the recipient one from real life issues, and make one vulnerable to disastrous accidents and life-events.

NATHAN: This is the opposite of the function of biblical parables which teach you to better cope with real life issues.

ALEC: What is a parable ?

NATHAN: It is a naked truth dressed up in beautiful clothing, making it easier to for people to take the underlying message into their hearts.

ALEC: Why?

NATHAN: The nakedness of truth frightens people.

ALEC: I never thought of it this way? Can you give us an example of a parable?

NATHAN: Yes, my encounter with David.

ALEC: Who is David?

NATHAN: He was King of Israel.

ALEC: What is the story?

NATHAN: David saw the beautiful Bathsheba bathing naked in a pool.

ALEC: And?

NATHAN: David summoned her to him and slept with her.

ALEC: Did he marry her?

NATHAN: She was already married—to Uriah, one of David's elite corps of soldiers.

ALEC: This is a very bad.

NATHAN: It gets worse.

ALEC: How?

NATHAN: She becomes pregnant by David.

ALEC: What does David do?

NATHAN: David summons Uriah home from the battlefield so that he will sleep with his wife

ALEC: So that Uriah would think the child would be his?

NATHAN: Yes. But Uriah refuses to go home to sleep with his wife- because he feels it would be disloyal to his men fighting on the battlefield.

ALEC: So, David's attempts to conceal his actions are frustrated.

NATHAN: Yes.

ALEC: So what does David do?

NATHAN: He sends Uriah back to the battlefield and arranges for him to be abandoned on a dangerous part of the battle-field to die.

ALEC: This is terrible.

NATHAN (to OEDIPUS): Yes it is, far worse than anything you have ever done, Oedipus.

ALEC: What did you do, Nathan?

NATHAN: God sent me to David to make him aware of the immorality of his actions.

ALEC: Did you tell him directly how wrong his actions were?

NATHAN: No, I was afraid to. Instead I told him a parable. It is a way of telling a truth, which allows a person to accept it.

ALEC: What parable did you tell him?

NATHAN: I told David the story of two men living in the same town, one was rich and the other poor. The rich man had sheep and cattle. And the poor man had nothing save one little ewe that whom he had nurtured from infancy.

ALEC: Please continue.

NATHAN: A wayfarer came to the rich man who used his power to take the poor man's ewe and slaughter it for the meal, rather than slaughter any of his many sheep and cattle.

ALEC: This is horrible. How did David react?

NATHAN: David became very angry towards the man.

ALEC: What did he say?

NATHAN: David's anger flared hot against the man. He said to me, "As the Lord lives, doomed is the man who has done this, and the poor man's ewe he shall pay back fourfold, in as much as he has done this thing, and because he has no pity!"[18]

ALEC: How did you respond?

NATHAN: I said to David: "You are the man!"

18. 2 Samuel 11-12.

ALEC: Did David become angry with you?

NATHAN: On the contrary. He admitted his sin and asked for forgiveness from the Lord.

ALEC: And how did your Lord respond?

NATHAN: I told him that the Lord had remitted his offense and he would not die. But that the son newly born to David and Bathsheba would die.

ALEC: Does their son die?

NATHAN: Yes. But after David grieves and atones, Bathsheba becomes pregnant again and begets another son, Solomon, who will succeed David as King of Israel.

ALEC: I see the power of a parable. It overcomes defenses.

NATHAN: Exactly, my dear Alec.

ISMENE: Let us continue this discussion next lesson.

Scene II-5. Ismene and Kallias meet again at the same café to discuss Oedipus's first class-and other things. They shyly express their growing feelings toward each other. Kallias expresses his frustration that Ismene is so tied to her father and that older men block younger men

KALLIAS: I have been impatient to meet you alone again.

ISMENE (blushing): Let us concentrate on the first lesson of my father.

KALLIAS (sheepishly): Of course.

ISMENE: How do you think it went?

KALLIAS: I think it went well.

ISMENE: Do you think the students understood what my father was saying?

KALLIAS: About riddles?

ISMENE: Yes, about riddles.

KALLIAS: I think they understood how ubiquitous riddles are in Greek society. I am not certain whether they fully understood how dangerous they can be.

ISMENE: I agree. I think in this next class; my father will give a more personal account on how he was done in by riddles.

KALLIAS: In what way?

ISMENE: He will tell the story of the way the Pythia did not answer the question that he asked her.

KALLIAS (touching ISMENE'S hand): And this led to the tragedy that befell your own family.

ISMENE (wiping away a tear in her eyes): Yes.

KALLIAS: I am here for you, Ismene.

ISMENE: Why do you say that?

KALLIAS: I have feelings for you, Ismene.

ISMENE: You are just saying this.

KALLIAS (somewhat angrily) : No, I am not just saying that. You are so tied to your father that you can't see anything else.

ISMENE: Of course I am tied to my father. He needs me and I need him. We have been estranged from each other for too long.

KALLIAS: Don't you want a life?

ISMENE: My father is my life.

KALLIAS: Don't you realize I have feelings for you? Don't you care for me at all?

ISMENE: Kallias, my father is my priority.

KALLIAS (*upset*): I need you also and your father is standing in our way; blocking our happiness. My father blocked me no matter how much I tried to please him, and now your father is doing the same thing. This is what older men do to younger men.

Kallias leaves the café angrily

Scene II-6. Oedipus teaches his second class regarding riddles with the help of Ismene and Kallias. Again Sophocles and Nathan are observers. They notice Kallias starting to act competitively with Oedipus. Kallias is asked to leave the classroom. Nathan is asked to construct a parable that would have helped Oedipus cope with his situation in a helpful way.

ISMENE: Today, my father will teach you about how damaging not having one's question answered directly can be. Can you tell us what happened to you, father?

OEDIPUS: Yes, I was at a dinner party when a drunken man questioned whether King Polybus and Queen Meirope of Corinth were my natural parents?

ISMENE: Did you believe him?

OEDIPUS: I was not sure.

ALEC: Had you ever questioned your lineage before?

OEDIPUS: No, of course not.

KALLIAS (interrupting): This was certainly foolish on your part, why would you believe such nonsense? Had Polybus and Meirope not been good to you?

OEDIPUS: They had been very good to me.

KALLIAS (pursuing his point): So you were being disloyal to them.

OEDIPUS: I wasn't being disloyal. I just wanted to be certain.

KALLIAS: I think you were being disloyal to them. Did you feel your father was blocking you?

ISMENE (nervously interrupting this exchange): What happened, next, father?

OEDIPUS: I went to my parents and asked them if the drunken man was correct in questioning my lineage.

KALLIAS: What did they answer, Oedipus?

OEDIPUS: That they were my natural parents.

KALLIAS (pressing ahead): So you stopped then?

OEDIPUS: No.

KALLIAS (pressing even further ahead): Why not, did you think that they would mislead you?

OEDIPUS: I just wanted to be certain.

ISMENE (again interrupting this exchange between Kallias and Oedipus): What happened, next, father?

OEDIPUS: I went to ask the Pythia who my parents were?

ALEC: Did she see you right away?

OEDIPUS: No, I had to go through a lengthy process.

ALEC: What was this process?

OEDIPUS: I met with priests who would determine whether my concern was genuine; and, moreover, how to frame my questions.

KALLIAS (provocatively): Why were you being so passive? Why didn't you insist on asking the question you wanted?

SOPHOCLES (interjecting): Because this was the procedure.

ALEC: So, were you able to ask your question at this point ?

OEDIPUS: No, I first carried a laurel wreath to the temple.

KALLIAS (laughing derisively): Why did you go along with all of this ?

SOPHOCLES: Because this was the procedure to see the Pythia. Why are you being so critical of Oedipus?

KALLIAS: Because he seemed to be acting like such a weakling.

ISMENE: I am not feeling well, and I need to leave. Excuse me for a moment.

(leaves the class temporarily)

SOPHOCLES (angrily): My dear Kallias, you seem to intention- ally misunderstand the process of being permitted to see the

Pythia. Your entire attitude towards Oedipus seems to have changed.

NATHAN: It seems that way to me also, Kallias.

KALLIAS (defensively): You are both mistaken. I am simply trying to understand what happened and draw a teaching lesson from it.

ALEC (to OEDIPUS): Did you now see the Pythia, dear sir?

OEDIPUS: No, I first had to provide a monetary donation and then present an animal to be sacrificed.

ALEC: Why was it important for an animal to be sacrificed?

OEDIPUS: Once the animal had been sacrificed, its guts would be studied. If the signs were seen as unfavorable, the consultant could be sent home.

ALEC: Without having a chance to ask the Pythia a question?

OEDIPUS: That is correct. However, the signs were favorable in my case.

ALEC: So now you could ask your question?

OEDIPUS: Yes.

KALLIAS (argumentatively): I would have demanded to ask my question. Why were you being so dependent?

SOPHOCLES (impatiently): Kallias, you know very well this is not the way the process works. It seems to me that you are just trying to pick at Oedipus, and it is very strange as you have been so helpful up to this point.

KALLIAS: I don't know what you mean.

NATHAN: Let us go on with the teaching. Can you continue with your story, Oedipus. what happened next?

OEDIPUS: I asked the Pythia the question as to who my father was and who was my mother.

ALEC: This was to answer the doubt that the drunken man had put in your head at the dinner party?

ISMENE (returning): Exactly.

ALEC: And what did the Pythia answer?

OEDIPUS: That when I grew up, I would kill my father and marry my mother.

SOPHOCLES (interjecting): And this is exactly what the Pythia told your father before you were born.

NATHAN: And this is why your father and mother tried to set you out in the field to die when you were born.

OEDIPUS: I thought King Polybus and Queen Meirope of Corinth were my natural parents and I fled Corinth to avoid hurting them.

ALEC: So this was the riddle.

ISMENE: Yes, this was the riddle. The identity of my father's natural parents.

ALEC: And what happened next ?

OEDIPUS: I fled from Corinth as quickly as I could, but on the road to Thebes I killed a man with whom I had an altercation at the crossing in the road.

ALEC: And who was this man?

OEDIPUS: My natural father, Laius.

ALEC: But you did not know this.

OEDIPUS: Of course not.

KALLIAS (sarcastically): Maybe you did and maybe you didn't.

ISMENE (angrily): Of course, my father did not know this! Please leave this class session until you can behave yourself better.

Kallias stalks out of the classroom.

ALEC: So, what happened next?

OEDIPUS: As I journeyed on towards Thebes, I encountered the Sphinx.

ALEC: I have heard of the Sphinx. She was a monster of sort who devoured people, was she not?

OEDIPUS: A fearsome monster perched on the top of the cliff. It was a strange creature, with the face of a woman, the body of a lion, and with wings like a huge bird. People were very frightened of her.

ALEC: What did this Sphinx do?

OEDIPUS: She asked passers-by a riddle. If they could not answer the riddle, the creature would swoop down and devour them.

ALEC: This must have been very frightening.

OEDIPUS: It was.

ALEC: What did you do?

OEDIPUS: I answered her riddles.

ALEC: Riddles? Were there more than one?

OEDIPUS: There were two.

ALEC: Do you remember them?

OEDIPUS: Yes.

ALEC: Can you tell them to us?

OEDIPUS: The first was: "Which creature has one voice and yet becomes four-footed and two-footed and three-footed?"

ALEC: What did you answer?

OEDIPUS: Man, who crawls on all fours as an infant, walks on two legs as an adult, and with the help of a cane as an elder.

ALEC: This was a brilliant answer. Was there a second riddle?

OEDIPUS: Yes.

ALEC: Can you tell us what it was?

OEDIPUS: "There are two sisters. One gives birth to the other and she, in turn, gives birth to the first. Who are the two sisters?"

ALEC: What did you answer?

OEDIPUS: Day and night, day giving birth to night and then night giving birth to day.

ALEC: This is ingenious. What happened next?

OEDIPUS: The Sphinx hurled itself down from the cliff and died.

ALEC: These were very clever responses.

OEDIPUS (ironically): They were so clever that they did me in.

ALEC: How?

OEDIPUS: I was given the widow of King Laius of Thebes as a wife.

ALEC: Who was this?

OEDIPUS: Queen Jocasta.

ALEC: This was an honor, no?

OEDIPUS: An honor? It was a horror!

ALEC: Why?

OEDIPUS: She was my mother.

ALEC: But you thought Queen Merope of Corinth was your mother.

OEDIPUS (sobbing): Of course, do you think that I would knowingly marry my mother?

ALEC: And then what happened?

OEDIPUS: A pestilence fell upon Thebes.

ALEC: Why?

OEDIPUS: Because the murderer of Laius was in Thebes.

ALEC: But you didn't know that you had killed Laius.

OEDIPUS (howling): Of course not. I was trying to avoid doing this. This is why I fled from Corinth where I thought my natural father was.

ALEC: Did you ask anyone to help uncover the source of the pestilence?

OEDIPUS: Yes, I consulted with our blind prophet Teiresias, but he just taunted me with dark riddles and made things worse.

ALEC (to NATHAN): Do you think you might have told him a parable that might have helped Oedipus understand his situation?

NATHAN: Yes, I thought of one that I think might have helped.

ALEC: Can you tell it to our class?

NATHAN: There was a man who was told he was going to kill the lamb he had raised from its youth and eat it.

ALEC: Go on.

NATHAN: To avoid doing this, he gave the lamb to a shepherd to guard it from being slaughtered.

ALEC: And?

NATHAN: But the shepherd suffered financial failures and had to sell the lamb to a butcher.

ALEC: Without telling the first man?

NATHAN: Yes, without telling the first man.

ALEC: I hear where this is going.

NATHAN: And the first man went to the butcher and bought the lamb and slaughtered it and ate it.

ALEC: Without realizing that it was his lamb.

NATHAN: Yes, without realizing it was his lamb. He had tried to protect his lamb

ALEC (to OEDIPUS): Isn't this what happened to you, esteemed sir?

OEDIPUS (sighing): Yes. I tried to avoid killing my father.

NATHAN: And if Teiresias had told you this story and concluded with informing you that you were this man. Might you not have accepted it?

OEDIPUS: Perhaps.

SOPHOCLES: And not taken your eyes out?

OEDIPUS: Perhaps not, but I did. But I have Ismene; she is my life.

ISMENE: Let us stop now. I think we have illustrated how parables can be helpful while riddles are often destructive.

ALEC: You most certainly have. I think we have learned something very important.

Scene II-7. Ismene and Kallias meet again at the same café and argue heatedly over what happened in Oedipus's second class-and other things. They ultimately express their love for each other and kiss for the first time. Kallias insists Oedipus will be able to go it alone in Thebes. Ismene refuses to leave her father. They part with the issue unresolved.

ISMENE: I don't know why I agreed to meet you. You acted terribly.

KALLIAS: I know.

ISMENE: Why did you act this way to my father in this last class? You have always been so kind to him.

KALLIAS: Because he is blocking our happiness.

ISMENE (angrily): No, it is you who are blocking our happiness, and you don't see it.

KALLIAS: How? I want to be with you.

ISMENE: You are so full of yourself that you don't see me, or understand what I want and need.

KALLIAS: Do you love me?

ISMENE: What has that got to do with it?

KALLIAS: Do you love me?

ISMENE (shouting): Yes, I love you, but you are a blockhead. I don't like you right now.

Kallias stands up from his chair and walks over to Ismene and kisses her. At first she resists but then she responds.

KALLIAS: I love you and I want you to be with me.

ISMENE: I will not leave my father. I am all he has.

KALLIAS: I will help him develop his course, and then he will be able to do it alone.

ISMENE: No, Kallias. I will never leave my father again.

Scene II-8. Ismene comes distraught to Sophocles' room to meet alone with Sophocles and Nathan.

SOPHOCLES: What brings you to meet with us, dear Ismene?

ISMENE (crying): I am very unhappy.

NATHAN: Why are you unhappy, dear child?

ISMENE: It is Kallias. I despise him.

SOPHOCLES: Despise him? Why? You seem to get along so well.

NATHAN: And he has helped you and your father so much.

ISMENE: He does not care about my father. He is selfish and arrogant and thinks only of himself.

SOPHOCLES: I must admit that he was very critical of your father during the second class.

NATHAN: So much so, that you ordered Kallias to leave the class.

ISMENE: Yes, do you blame me for this?

SOPHOCLES: No, I was shocked myself by Kallias's behavior as it was so out of character for him. He comes from a very fine family and his father Theodectes is a very successful playwright and my dear friend.

NATHAN (tenderly): What happened, dear child?

ISMENE: Kallias doesn't care about my father.

NATHAN: Why do you say this?

ISMENE: Because Kallias wants me to leave my father.

SOPHOCLES: Why does Kallias want this?

ISMENE: Because he wants me for himself.

NATHAN: He wants to marry you?

ISMENE: Yes.

NATHAN: Do you love him?

ISMENE: I hate him.

NATHAN: But do you love him?

ISMENE: Yes, unfortunately.

SOPHOCLES: This is wonderful, Ismene, you should be happy, not sad. Kallias comes from a wonderful family

ISMENE: But Kallias has never felt he could measure up to his father.

NATHAN: I can see that you do love Kallias, dear Ismene. So, what is the problem?

ISMENE (crying): He wants me to leave my father and marry him.

NATHAN: I see the problem, dear Ismene. You feel very loyal to your father.

ISMENE: My father needs me, and we have finally reunited after the terrible things that happened to our family.

NATHAN: You are both survivors. Is that how you feel, Ismene?

ISMENE: Yes. I will never leave him again.

SOPHOCLES: But you have a right to your own life, Ismene. You deserve it.

ISMENE: That doesn't help, Sophocles. I know you are trying to make me feel better, but I will never leave my father again.

NATHAN (softly): And you don't think Kallias understands how you feel?

ISMENE: No, he doesn't. He just doesn't care. All he cares about is himself. He has problems with his own father, and doesn't trust older men.

NATHAN: Please do not make any decisions, Ismene. Let me meet alone with Sophocles and we will discuss the situation.

ISMENE: I am so miserable.

NATHAN: I know, my child. (to Sophocles) Can you and I meet tomorrow morning?

SOPHOCLES: Of course.

Scene II-9. Nathan and Sophocles make plans to invite the biblical judge and prophetess Deborah and the Greek historian Hesiod to come to Oedipus's class to discuss the relationship of father and son, and also how to treat an aging parent.

NATHAN: We have a real problem.

SOPHOCLES: Yes, I can see that we do.

NATHAN: Actually, I think we have several problems.

SOPHOCLES: Several?

NATHAN: First, the problem of the rivalry of father and son.

SOPHOCLES: Yes,

NATHAN: We have a story that speaks to that.

SOPHOCLES: So do we.

NATHAN: Other than that between Oedipus and his father? — which is more about mistaken identity caused by misleading riddles than anything else.

SOPHOCLES: Yes, we have a full-blown rivalry discussed by our chronicler Hesiod in his *Theogony*.

NATHAN: Who is it between?

SOPHOCLES: It is between Uranus and his son Cronus, and between Cronus and his son Zeus.

NATHAN: Can you arrange for Hesiod to come into the next class?

SOPHOCLES: Not to the next class. I will need a little time.

NATHAN: We also have a story of the relationship between father and son.

SOPHOCLES: What story is this?

NATHAN: That between Abraham and Isaac.

SOPHOCLES. Can you get someone to come in to discuss it?

NATHAN: Yes, I think I can ask the prophetess and judge Deborah to come in. She was of help in a similar situation.

SOPHOCLES: That is good. We will need permission from Oedipus to bring these figures in.

NATHAN: I will leave this to you and Ismene.

SOPHOCLES: We should be able to bring this about.

NATHAN: I think Deborah can discuss perhaps an even more relevant story.

SOPHOCLES: What story is that?

NATHAN: The story of Ruth and her aging mother-in-law Naomi.

SOPHOCLES: How will this story help? What is this story about?

NATHAN: You will see.

SOPHOCLES: How much time will you need?

NATHAN: About a month.

SOPHOCLES: We can help run a class for Oedipus before that focusing on the limits of vision and the ways in which hearing can actually be superior.

NATHAN: Yes, we can help Oedipus and Ismene run this class, but I do not think Kallias should be part of it.

SOPHOCLES: I agree, he should stay away from this next class and only return when we bring in Hesiod and Deborah.

NATHAN: I agree.

Scene II-10. Oedipus teaches his third class with the help of Ismene regarding sight versus insight. Sophocles and Nathan are present but Kallias is absent. Nathan discusses the story of Samson as he knows it and that of the biblical God choosing the youngest shepherd boy David to be King of Israel.

ISMENE: Welcome again, students. Today my father will talk to you about seeing and hearing, and how he has adjusted to the loss of his outer sight.

OEDIPUS: Thank you, dear daughter. Today I want to tell you about how I lost my sight and how I have learned to live with this. My assistant, Kallias will help me teach this along with my daughter, and Sophocles and Nathan will comment in this regard.

ISMENE: Kallias will not be at this class, father. He does not feel well.

OEDIPUS: He did seem to be acting unwell in the last class. Anyhow we will proceed without him.

ALEC: How did you lose your vision, my dear sir?

OEDIPUS (sharply): I said I lost my sight, young man. I did not say I lost my vision. There is a big difference.

ISMENE (softly): Alec did not mean any harm, father. Please tell the class your story.

OEDIPUS: After I realized what I had done, I was very ashamed to see my parents in the netherworld and I took out my eyes.

ALEC: And what had you done that was so terrible, esteemed sir?

OEDIPUS: You know what I had done, young man. Don't taunt me. I had killed my father and married and bedded my mother.

ALEC: But you were trying to avoid doing this. You taught us in the last class that you were entrapped by a riddle. The Pythia did not answer your question as to who your natural parents were.

ISMENE: Alec is trying to help you, father.

OEDIPUS: But at that time, I did not realize this, and I blamed myself.

ISMENE: And you took out your eyes, father.

OEDIPUS: And I took out my eyes, daughter and I was wandering alone outside of Thebes when Nathan found me. Is this not correct, Nathan?

NATHAN: Yes, my dear man.

OEDIPUS: In any case, I was blind, and could not see, and I did not want to live.

ALEC: Even when you realized you had been entrapped and were not guilty of intentionally killing your natural father and marrying your natural mother.

OEDIPUS (ironically): Especially after I realized I had had been entrapped by the riddling answer of the Pythia.

ALEC: Why? If you had come to realize you were innocent.

OEDIPUS: Especially when I came to realize I was innocent.

ALEC: Why, if you knew you were innocent?

OEDIPUS: Then why had I taken out my eyes?

ALEC: So, what happened. What made you want to live again?.

OEDIPUS: Several things. First, I became reunited with my daughter Ismene, and this means everything to me.

ISMENE (blurting in): It means everything to me also, father.

ALEC: What is the second thing?

OEDIPUS: I began to realize that inner sight (indeed *insight*) can sometimes be more important than outer sight. Do you understand that? And also that one can be betrayed by one's eyes.

ALEC: I think maybe a little bit. What made you understand that?

OEDIPUS: The story of Samson told by the Judeans in Jerusalem. It was told to me by the Hebrew prophetess and judge Deborah.

ALEC: What is this story?

OEDIPUS: Manoah and his wife are childless. One day, an angel of God appeared to Manoah's wife promising that she will bear a son who will save the Israelites from the Philistines. They named him Samson.

ALEC: Who are the Israelites and who are the Philistines, Oedipus?

NATHAN (interjecting): I am an Israelite, Alec. I live in Judea across the Mediterranean Sea and believe in one invisible God that rules all. The Philistines did not believe in our God and were our enemies and tried to subjugate us.

ALEC: But where did these Philistines come from?

SOPHOCLES: The Philistines were descendants of the Phoenicians, themselves a sea people. who likely came from Greece and spoke Greek.

NATHAN: Samson was our champion, Alec. He was champion of the Israelites and he was given immense strength as long as he never cut his hair.

ALEC: If he had such immense strength, what did he do?

NATHAN: He was able to kill a lion. slay an entire army with only the jawbone of an ass, and destroy a temple of the Philistines with his bare hands.

ALEC: He is like our Heracles. Were there any conditions?

NATHAN: Yes, Samson's mother was told she could not con-
taminate her body with any alcohol, because her child,
Samson, will be a Nazirite—dedicated to God from birth.
She also learns that her son will save the Israelites from the
Philistines.[19]

ALEC: Where there any other conditions?

NATHAN: Yes, one very important one.

ALEC: What was that?

NATHAN: Samson must never cut his hair or he will lose his immense strength.[20]

ALEC: So this seems simple. Samson never should cut his hair.

NATHAN: It proved to not be that simple.

ALEC: Why not?

OEDIPUS: Because of Samson's weakness in "following his eyes."

ALEC: What do you mean?

OEDIPUS: Samson "follows his eyes" in lusting after Philistine
women rather than his own Israelite women.[21]

ALEC: I don't understand.

OEDIPUS: Samson first asks his father to bring him a Philistine
woman he has lusted after to be his wife.[22]

---

19. Judges 13.
20. Judges 13:5.
21. Judges 14.
22. Judges 14:1.

ALEC: Does his father object?

OEDIPUS: Yes, both his parents do. They want him to find a wife among the Israelites.[23]

ALEC: What happens?

OEDIPUS: A very strange story. On his way to claim this non-Israelite bride, Samson discovers his super-human strength: A young lion roars at him, and he tears the lion apart.[24]

ALEC: And then?

OEDIPUS: Samson uses this strength to kill thirty Philistine men in a fit of rage.[25]

ALEC: Why was Samson so angry?

OEDIPUS: He had difficulty controlling his temper. He was very impulsive, but he had superhuman strength.

ALEC: What happened next?

OEDIPUS: The Philistines raid a town in Judah in order to lure and capture Samson. To save themselves, the Judeans tie up Samson to deliver him to the enemy.

ALEC: So, his people betray Samson? Do they succeed?

OEDIPUS: No. Samson found a fresh jaw-bone of a donkey, reached down and took it, and with it he killed a thousand of the Philistines.[26]

ALEC: He really is like our Heracles.

23. Judges 14:2.
24. Judges 14:6.
25. Judges 14:19.
26. Judges 15:9–16.

SOPHOCLES: Yes, but remember that our Hera had no love for Heracles. She saw him as a product of her husband's infidelity.

ALEC: This is such an interesting story.

NATHAN (interjecting): A very sad story in some ways.

ALEC: Why?

OEDIPUS: Samson 'follows his eyes" and becomes involved with a second Philistine woman–the notorious Delilah, who has been tasked by her people to find the secret of Samson's strength.

ALEC: Does she succeed?

OEDIPUS: Ultimately yes.

NATHAN (again interjecting): Three times Delilah begs to know the secret of his strength, and three times Samson lies to her. Finally, after Delilah nags persistently, he confesses: "A razor has never come to my head; for I have been a Nazarite to God from my mother's womb. If my head were shaved, then my strength would leave me"[27]

ALEC: What did Delilah do?

NATHAN: Delilah lulls Samson to sleep and shaves off his hair. He immediately weakens, and God's power leaves him. Delilah hands Samson over to the Philistines, who gouge out his eyes, and force him to grind at a mill in prison.[28]

OEDIPUS: Samson is done in by his lust for Delilah?

ALEC: He is done in by his eyes.

27. Judges 16:17
28. Judges 16:18–23.

NATHAN: Yes, but his blindness ends up leading to his greatest victory against the Philistines.

ALEC: How could this be? What happened?

OEDIPUS: The Philistines think Samson's blindness has left him helpless and harmless.

ALEC: Are they right?

OEDIPUS: No, they have not taken into account that his hair has grown back.

ALEC: So what do they do?

OEDIPUS: The Philistines bring Samson down to Gaza and bind him to two pillars in their temple at Dagon as a display for the amusement of the Philistine worshipers.

ALEC: What does Samson do?

NATHAN: Samson prays to God, asking for his strength to return to him one more time God responds by sending Samson a final burst of strength, and Samson pushes against the pillars and brings the entire temple down, killing himself and all those in the temple with him. The text concludes: "Those he killed at his death were more than those he had killed during his life"[29]

ALEC: So his blindness actually leads to his greatest triumph?

NATHAN: Yes, in a strange way. The Philistines believe the loss of his sight has made him impotent, but they are wrong.

ALEC: What do you mean?

29. Judges 16:28–20.

NATHAN: That Samson is now free from the distractions and pitfalls to which his eyes have led him and can concentrate on his life mission: to fight for the Israelites.

ALEC: Are you saying that Samson was actually freed by the loss of his eyesight?

NATHAN: Yes, in a way. It says in our holy book the following: "And the Lord spoke unto Moses, saying: 'Speak unto the children of Israel, and bid them that they make them throughout their generations fringes in the corners of their garments, and that they put with the fringe of each corner a thread of blue." [30]

ALEC (interrupting): I don't understand.

NATHAN: The passage continues: "And it shall be unto you for a fringe, that ye may look upon it, and remember all the commandments of the Lord, and do them; and that ye go not about after your own heart and your own eyes, after which ye use to go astray . . . "[31]

ALEC (incredulously): Are you saying losing your eyesight is a good thing in the Hebrew tradition ?

NATHAN: In a way, it frees one up to "see" more deeply.

ALEC: What are you saying?

OEDIPUS (inserting): That sometimes losing one's sight give one a deeper insight. That moral vision is more important than physical sight.

---

30 Numbers 15:37–38.

31. Numbers 15:39–40.

NATHAN: Indeed, our tradition debates the true character of Samson. saying that Samson's eyes were gouged out as punishment for having followed the desires of his eyes.[32]

ALEC: Is there anything in my Greek tradition that would believe this, that blindness is preferable to sight?

SOPHOCLES (interjecting): Yes, there is.

ALEC: Where?

SOPHOCLES: In the soothsayer Teiresias's response to you, Oedipus. Do you remember it?

OEDIPUS: Please remind me.

SOPHOCLES: Remember, the city of Thebes was suffering a great pestilence.

ALEC: I have heard of that. Why was it having this pestilence?

SOPHOCLES: Because it was polluted by the murderer of King Laius being in the boundaries of the city.

ALEC: Go on.

SOPHOCLES: Oedipus, do you remember summoning the blind prophet Teiresias to help shed light on the issue.

OEDIPUS: I do, vaguely. I wanted to understand the reason for the plague on this city.

SOPHOCLES: Do you remember what he said ?

OEDIPUS: Yes, he said that the murderer of King Laius was in Thebes and a pollutant on the land.

SOPHOCLES: Do you remember how you reacted?

32. *Babylonian Talmud*, Sotah 9b

OEDIPUS: Yes, I became very angry with him.

ALEC: Why, esteemed sir, did you become so angry with him?

OEDIPUS: Because he was speaking to me in riddles. He told me I myself was the man I was looking for.

SOPHOCLES: Do you remember what you said to him?

OEDIPUS: Yes, it is coming back to me now. I told him that truth was not in him for his ears and his mind, as well as his eyes were blind.[33]

SOPHOCLES: Do you remember how he answered?

OEDIPUS: I think that he called me a wretched fool and that I would soon be blind as well.

ALEC: Oh my, how did you respond, esteemed sir?

OEDIPUS: I don't remember exactly.

SOPHOCLES: You told him that since he lived in "an endless darkness of the night," he could never injure you or any man.

ALEC: This is terrible. How did he respond, esteemed sir?

OEDIPUS: He told me that although I had my eyesight, I did not see, and how miserable my own living situation was.

ALEC: How did you respond, esteemed sir.

OEDIPUS: I banished him from Thebes, but he turned out to be correct.[34]

ALEC: How was he correct?

---

33. Sophocles, *Oedipus the King*, lines 370–71.

34. Sophocles, *Oedipus the King*, lines 298-460

OEDIPUS: Because my eyes blinded me to my real situation.

ALEC: Like Samson, you were following your eyes.

OEDIPUS: Like Samson, I was following my eyes.

NATHAN: There is no question that in the Jewish tradition we say, "Hear O Israel (*Shema Yisrael*)" and not "See O Israel."[35]

ALEC: This is so interesting. Are there any other examples in the Hebrew tradition?

NATHAN: The prophet Samuel being sent by God to Jesse the Bethlehemite to choose a successor to King Saul from among Jesse's sons.

ALEC: Go on. Can you tell us what happens?

NATHAN: Samuel first beheld Eliab, Jesse's eldest son, who looked very much the part of a king.

ALEC: And?

NATHAN: But God rejects him.

ALEC: Why?

NATHAN: Because of what the Lord says to Samuel.

ALEC: What does your god say?

NATHAN: "Look not on his countenance , or on the height of his stature; because I have rejected him: for it is not as man seeth: for man looketh on the outward appearance, but the Lord looketh on the heart."[36]

ALEC: Does your god reject all of Jesse's sons?

35. Deuteronomy 6:4.
36. Samuel 1, 16: 6-7.

NATHAN: No, he rejects all of Jesse's seven oldest sons, but upon Samuel's insistence, Jesse sends his youngest son David, who has been keeper of the sheep.

ALEC: And?

NATHAN: And it is this son, David, that Samuel chooses to anoint as the future king of Israel.

OEDIPUS: So the god of the Jews sees with an inner eye.

ALEC: What do all these stories mean?

OEDIPUS: That people can be led astray by their eyes.

NATHAN: Even betrayed by them.

ISMENE: There is much to absorb here, Alec.

ALEC: Much.

ISMENE: Let us end this class now.

Scene II-11. Ismene comes into her father Oedipus's room and tearfully tells him of her love for Kallias. Oedipus expresses his fear of being abandoned.

ISMENE: Hello, father.

OEDIPUS: Is that you, my daughter?

ISMENE (crying): Yes, father?

OEDIPUS: Are you crying, Ismene?

ISMENE: No . . . Yes.

OEDIPUS: Why are you crying, my dearest daughter? I cannot bear to hear your unhappiness.

ISMENE: It is nothing, father.

OEDIPUS: So why then are you crying?

ISMENE: I am not crying!

OEDIPUS: So then things are good?

ISMENE (sighs): Yes. No.

OEDIPUS: Did you think the last class was powerful?

ISMENE (still sighing): Yes, very powerful.

OEDIPUS: I thought it was very strange that Kallias was not at the last class.

ISMENE: It was not so strange, father.

OEDIPUS: I have noticed he has started behaving aggressively towards me.

ISMENE: He has not been himself.

OEDIPUS: Did he upset you, daughter?

ISMENE (breaking into tears): No. Yes.

OEDIPUS (embracing his daughter): What is going on, my dearest daughter?

ISMENE: He is horrible, father.

OEDIPUS: Who is horrible?

ISMENE: Kallias.

OEDIPUS: Kallias? I thought you like him, Ismene.

ISMENE: I hate him.

OEDIPUS: Hate him? I didn't know that. Then we will stop working with him and send him away. The important thing is that we have each other, dearest daughter.

ISMENE: Yes . . . No . . . I don't want to send him away.

OEDIPUS: Why not? If you hate him.

ISMENE: Don't you understand, father?

OEDIPUS: I am afraid I don't, dearest daughter.

ISMENE: I love him, father.

OEDIPUS: You love him? I just hear you say you hated him. I am getting confused.

ISMENE: Don't you understand, father, I hate him because I love him.

OEDIPUS: You hate him because you love him. You are really confusing me. Do you love him or hate him and why are you so miserable. Does he not love you?

ISMENE: No, he does love me. Don't you see?

OEDIPUS: You know I am blind, daughter.

ISMENE: Listen to me, father.

OEDIPUS: So, you love him, and he loves you. What is the problem, daughter? I am more confused.

ISMENE: You are not hearing me.

OEDIPUS: What do you want me to hear?

ISMENE: He wants me to marry him.

OEDIPUS (suddenly realizing the situation): You won't leave me alone, daughter, will you?

ISMENE (sobbing uncontrollably): You know I won't.

OEDIPUS (also crying): You won't leave me alone again, will you daughter?

Scene II-12. A month later. Nathan arrives to a café with the biblical prophetess and judge Deborah. Sophocles is already sitting at a table with the Greek chronicler Hesiod. Introductions are made and a plan is developed for their joint appearance at a special class of and for Oedipus, Ismene and Kallias.

NATHAN: Good morning, Sophocles. I have brought Deborah who has come all the way from Judea to help us.

SOPHOCLES: It is very good that you have come, Deborah, we have a bit of a problem on our hands. And I have bought our famous chronicler, Hesiod.

NATHAN: I am honored that you have come, dear Hesiod. I have heard of you.

HESIOD: I know a little of the situation and want to help if I can. Can you lay it out a bit more?

SOPHOCLES: What has happened is that Ismene and Kallias have fallen in love with each other.

HESIOD: That is wonderful.

SOPHOCLES: Not exactly.

HESIOD: Why not?

SOPHOCLES: Kallias seems to feel jealous of Oedipus, the father of Ismene.

HESIOD: It is the theme of our creation story.

SOPHOCLES: And Oedipus is jealous of Kallias.

HESIOD: Of course, it works both ways.

SOPHOCLES: Can you talk about this problem in a special class that Oedipus, Ismene and Kallias are conducting.

HESIOD: I can. I will illustrate it with the story of Uranus, Gaia and Cronus in my *Theogony*.

NATHAN: What is this story?

HESIOD: It is the story of mother earth Gaia colluding with her son Cronus to castrate his father Uranus.

NATHAN: Oh my. Do you really have such a story?

HESIOD: We do. Will you protect me from Kallias or Oedipus throwing parchment at me?

SOPHOCLES (laughing): Of course. Nathan, can you introduce the prophetess Deborah, whom I have met before.

NATHAN: This is Deborah, the great biblical judge and prophetess.

SOPHOCLES: Welcome, Deborah.

DEBORAH: Thank you, dear Sophocles.

NATHAN: Do you have any stories in our biblical tradition that you can speak about that will treat the rivalry between Oedipus and Kallias?

DEBORAH: Yes, I think I may have two actually.

NATHAN: What are they?

DEBORAH: First, we have the story of Abraham's circumcision of Isaac, our *brit hamilah*, and also the command of the father to teach his son thoroughly.

SOPHOCLES: What is this *brit hamilah*?

NATHAN: It is our practice of the father circumcising his son, the cutting away of the foreskin of the penis. This is aimed at overcoming the rivalry of father and son.

SOPHOCLES: This sounds like castration.

NATHAN: No, it is the opposite.

SOPHOCLES: You said you might have a second story, Deborah. What is the other one?

DEBORAH: It is the story of Ruth and her mother-in-law Naomi, but I am not certain if it will be relevant.

NATHAN: We will see.

SOPHOCLES: We will hold this special class next week at this time. There will be twelve students in the class, led by their leader Alec.

NATHAN: Very good.

Scene II-13. Kallias returns to the class. Ismene sits between him and Oedipus. Sophocles brings in Hesiod to discuss the rivalry between Cronus and his father expressed in the Greek creation story. Nathan brings in the prophetess Deborah to tell the biblical story of Abraham circumcising his son Isaac.

ISMENE (nervously): Welcome to this special class. We will discuss a topic of great importance here. The relationship between father and son. Or perhaps more generally, the relationship between older man and younger man.

ALEC: Thank you, Ismene. This should be a very interesting class.

OEDIPUS (nervously): This is a topic we had not originally planned to cover.

ALEC: Welcome back, Kallias.

KALLIAS (cautiously): Thank you.

SOPHOCLES: I have asked our great chronicler Hesiod to start this class by telling us the Creation Story in his *Theogony*. Welcome, esteemed sir.

The class applauds, led by Alec. Oedipus and Kallias remain silent.

HESIOD: Thank you, my dear Sophocles. Let me summarize our *Theogony*.

ALEC: What is a "theogony?"

HESIOD: It is an account of the origin and descent of the gods.

NATHAN: The Greek gods.

HESIOD (smiling): Are there any others?

SOPHOCLES (purposely ignoring this exchange): Proceed with your summary, esteemed sir.

HESIOD: Our Theogony begins with *Chaos*.

ALEC: What is "chaos."

HESIOD: Nothingness? Out of this Chaos, the first beings were born. These beings were Gaia (or, Mother Earth), Eros (desire), Tartarus (the underworld), Erebus (darkness), and Nyx (night).

ALEC: This is starting to sound familiar. Please continue.

HESIOD: In a virgin-birth, Gaia created Uranus— the sky, or heavens. From Gaia and Uranus, the twelve Titans, three Cyclopes, and three hecatonchiries were born.

ALEC: What are hecatonchiries?

HESIOD: Hundred-headed monsters.

ALEC: Go on. What did Uranus do?

HESIOD: Uranus hated the hecatoncheries and banished them to Tartarus.

ALEC: How did Gaia react?

HESIOD: As you might imagine, she was devastated by Uranus's actions.

ALEC: What did Gaia do?

HESIOD: She asked Kronos, one of the Titans, to dethrone Uranus. Using a sickle made of adamant gifted to him by Gaia, Kronos castrated Uranus and successfully dethroned him.

ALEC: Castrated him. This is terrible. A son castrating his father! Is this the end of this terrible story?

HESIOD: No. It continues. From Uranus's blood, the Furies, Giants, and Meliai are born. Kronos threw Uranus's genitals into the sea, from which Aphrodite goddess of love, was born. Kronos and his wife, Rhea, ascended to the throne as king and queen of the gods.

ALEC: So it ends here, I hope, and that things do become more peaceful.

HESIOD: Alas, no. Kronos and Rhea had six children: Hestia, Demeter, Hera, Hades, Poseidon, and Zeus. There was a prophecy that one of Kronos' children would overthrow him as he had his own father, and in order to prevent this, Kronos ate each of his children as they were born.

ALEC: And how did Rhea react?

HESIOD: Rhea was understandably upset and horrified by Kronos' actions.

ALEC: I should think so. But what did she do?

HESIOD: She prevented Kronos from eating her youngest child, Zeus, by giving Kronos a rock disguised as a baby in his place. In order to avoid being found by Kronos, Rhea hid Zeus on Mount Ida.

ALEC: I feel like vomiting.

HESIOD: It is funny you say that, because that is exactly what happened.

ALEC: What do you mean?

HESIOD: Once Zeus had matured and grown strong enough, he embarked to avenge his siblings and defeat Kronos. Disguising himself, Zeus forced Kronos into vomiting up his siblings by giving him a poisoned drink.

ALEC: And then?

HESIOD: Alongside his siblings, the Cyclopes, and the Titans (Prometheus and Epimetheus), Zeus fought against Kronos and his allies: the Giants.

ALEC: Did Zeus win?

HESIOD: After a ten-year battle, Kronos was defeated, and Zeus and Hera ascended to the throne as the new and final rulers of the gods.[37]

ALEC: This is a terrible view of the father-son relationship.

SOPHOCLES: And it goes on from generation to generation.

OEDIPUS: And this is what happened to me, Alec. My father thought I would kill him when I "reached man's estate" and marry my mother. Thus he sent me out to die in the fields as an infant.

ISMENE: Look at your own insecurity and jealousy with regard to Kallias, father. And how you reacted when I told you I loved him.

KALLIAS: Fi-nal-ly.

ISMENE : You are no better, Kallias. Look at how you have been jealous of my father.

KALLIAS: He is trying to keep you from being with me. He is jealous of me.

---

37. Hesiod, The Library of Apollodorus, 1.1–1.7.

OEDIPUS: I am not jealous of you, Kallias. You were a friend to me, and now you are acting like my enemy.

ISMENE: Enough from both of you. Is there no better way for an older man and younger man to relate to each other?

DEBORAH: Yes, there is, in our tradition. The story of our patriarch Abraham and his son, Isaac.

ALEC: Can you tell it to us?

DEBORAH: Our Holy Torah tells us the following story. "And the LORD visited Sarah as he had said, and the LORD did unto Sarah as he had spoken. For Sarah conceived, and bore Abraham a son in his old age, at the set time of which God had spoken to him".[38]

ALEC: Was Abraham jealous of his son like Kronus was of his sons?

DEBORAH: No, seemingly the opposite.

ALEC: How do we know this?

DEBORAH: Because of how Abraham acted.

ALEC: And *how* did Abraham act?

DEBORAH: Abraham called the name of his son that was born unto him, whom Sarah bore to him, Isaac. And Abraham circumcised his son Isaac being eight days old, as God had commanded him.[39]

ALEC: What is this "circumcision"?

---

38. Genesis 21:1–2.
39. Genesis 21:3–4.

DEBORAH: It is the cutting off the foreskin of the penis of the baby Isaac.

ALEC: This sounds very much like castration to me.

DEBORAH (emphatically): No, circumcision in our tradition is called *brit-ha-mila*. It is designed to overcome the terrible conflict between fathers and sons so omnipresent in your Greek tradition.

ALEC: How does it do this?

NATHAN (interjecting): May I answer Alec, Deborah?

DEBORAH: Of course, esteemed prophet.

NATHAN: In our Torah, our God (*Ha Shem*) makes a covenant with Abraham and his descendants: God will bless Abraham and give him the land of Canaan as his own; in return, Abraham and his progeny will follow God's law.[40]

ALEC: Is there more?

NATHAN: Yes, The father is not the owner of his son nor does he hold the power of infant exposure as in your tradition.

ALEC: So how does *your* tradition see the relationship between father and son?

NATHAN: We see it in terms of the fulfillment of our covenant with HaShem. The child honors his father and mother as something that follows from his obedience to *Ha Shem*, not from personal obligation to the parent. The urge of father and son to destroy each other is superseded by the obligation of both to fulfill and continue the covenant.

ALEC: How does this play out, Nathan?

40. Genesis 17:9–11.

NATHAN: One of the most significant themes in our tradition is the commandment to the father to teach his children thoroughly.[41]

ALEC: So the father is not afraid of his son growing beyond him?

NATHAN: No, the father's identity is not threatened by the son. He wants to see his son develop and even surpass him.

ALEC: So the son does not learn that he is an unwanted burden?

NATHAN: Not at all, but that his well-being is beneficial both to God and to his father. He does not need to feel guilty for existing, nor does he entertain thoughts of self-destruction, even in his darkest hour.

ALEC: It is extraordinary that this is symbolized by circumcision that on the surface seems to be so similar to castration. Each generation is a link in the chain between the generation before and the generation after.

DEBORAH: This is exactly right, Alec. The father willingly passes down the covenant, making it unnecessary for his son to displace him.

NATHAN: Yes. The son becomes aware that the father could have castrated him and destroyed his power of procreation and creativity but chose not to.

ALEC: So what does the father do instead?

DEBORAH: The father offers a sanctified and non-injurious circumcision as the very symbol of his love and assent to the son's right to succession.

ALEC: And what does this accomplish?

41. Deut. 6:7; Kiddushin, 30a.

NATHAN: This relationship results in increased mutual security, making attacks by the father on the son or by the son on the father unnecessary.

DEBORAH: And this plays out throughout our tradition.

ALEC: How?

DEBORAH: Abraham goes through a series of tests, culminating in the binding of Isaac, what we call the *Akedah*.

ALEC: What is this *Akedah*?

DEBORAH: God's command to Abraham to sacrifice his son Isaac on our Mount Moriah.[42]

ALEC (totally engrossed): So what does Abraham do? Does he sacrifice Isaac?

DEBORAH: No, Abraham binds Isaac on the altar, but *Ha Shem* (our God) will not allow the sacrifice.

ALEC: How does your *ha shem* stop this?

DEBORAH: But the Angel of the Lord called to him from heaven and said, "Abraham, Abraham!" So he said, "Here I am." And He said, "Do not lay your hand on the lad, nor do anything to him; for now, I know that you fear God, since you have not withheld your son, your only son, from me.[43]

ALEC: So, this is the very opposite of the Greek theogony that you have told us, Hesiod.

HESIOD: It is.

---

42. Genesis 22
43. Genesis 22:11-12

NATHAN: Unlike the Greek earth- mother, the God of Genesis will never demand infanticide. Rather, full obedience to this God demands a rejection of these destructive tendencies. Abraham, Isaac, and all their descendants are released from the terrible forces create murderous rivalry between older and younger men that resonates through the Greek tradition.

ISMENE (to both Oedipus and Kallias): Do you hear this, both of you?

DEBORAH: I think I have several other stories that can help you all resolve your issue.

SOPHOCLES: Let us stop right now as we all have a lot to absorb, and meet again next week to hear this story, Deborah.

Scene II-14. The continuation of the past class begins the following week. Both Oedipus and Kallias expresses their fear of being abandoned. Deborah first tells Ismene, Kallias and Oedipus and the entire class the biblical story of Solomon determining which of two women was the mother of a dead infant, and which of a live infant. Oedipus and Kallias begin to reconcile after hearing this story. Deborah then tells Ismene, Kallias and Oedipus the biblical story of Ruth bringing her widowed mother-in-law Naomi into her home with her new husband Boaz and their son Obed. Oedipus and Kallias now fully reconcile and Oedipus gives his blessing for the wedding of Kallias and Ismene. They invite him to live in their home. The biblical story of God putting a rainbow in the sky after the great flood is celebrated as a symbol of hope and as an antidote to the Greek story of the first woman Pandora locking hope up in the urn given to her by Zeus after loosing all the evils into the world. They all celebrate.

ISMENE (somewhat shakily): Welcome again to the continuation of the last class. What exactly is it we want to cover today?

DEBORAH: Before we discuss this, it seems to me that that are some unresolved feelings going on, are there not?

KALLIAS: Yes, Oedipus who I have befriended is standing in the way of my marriage to Ismene.

DEBORAH: Is this the way you see this, Oedipus?

OEDIPUS: No, the opposite.

DEBORAH: What do you mean, "the opposite"?

OEDIPUS: Kallias, whom I have trusted and befriended is trying to convince my daughter to abandon me. He knows I only have recently reconciled with her and need her. He can see I am blind.

DEBORAH: Dear Oedipus and Kallias, will you let me tell you a story from my tradition that might help?

KALLIAS: If it will help, I am willing to listen. He is a stubborn old man.

OEDIPUS: I will listen, but he is a very ungrateful youth.

ISMENE (screaming): Be quiet, both of you! This isn't love. Neither one of you seems to care what I want. You think only of yourselves. Please tell us the story you mentioned, Deborah.

DEBORAH: The First Book of Kings states that Israel's great King Solomon was twelve years old when God promised him that he would be granted great wisdom.[44] He turned out to be the wisest man ever to live. As an illustration of the fulfillment of this blessing of wisdom, the Book of Kings reports the following account of a case that was brought before King Solomon's court in Jerusalem.

ISMENE: What was the case?

DEBORAH: Two women came to King Solomon and stood before him. One woman said: "My Lord, this woman and I dwell in the same house, and I gave birth to a child while with her in the house. On the third day after I gave birth, she also gave birth. We live together; there is no outsider with us in the house; only the two of us were there.

ISMENE: Please continue.

DEBORAH: The son of this woman died during the night because she lay upon him. She arose during the night and took my son from my side while I was asleep, and lay him in her bosom, and her dead son she laid in my bosom. when I got up in the morning to nurse my son, behold, he was dead! But when I observed him (later on) in the morning, I realized that he was not my son to whom I had given birth!"[45]

OEDIPUS: Was this woman telling the truth?

DEBORAH: Well, The other woman replied: "It is not so! My son is the live one and your son is the dead one!"[46]

KALLIAS: Was this woman then telling the truth?

---

44. I Kings 1. 3:12
45. I Kings 3:16-21.
46. I Kings 3:22.

DEBORAH: The first woman responded: "It is not so! Your son is the dead one and my son is the living one!" They took their argument to King Solomon.[47]

ISMENE: How did King Solomon rule?

DEBORAH: King Solomon said: "this second woman claims, 'My son is the live one and your son is the dead one, 'and the first woman claims, 'Your son is the dead one and my son is the living one!'"[48]

ISMENE (impatiently): But how did Solomon rule?

DEBORAH: King Solomon said, "Bring me a sword!" So they brought a sword before the King. The King said, "Cut the living child in two, and give half to one and half to the other."[49]

OEDIPUS: My god!!! This is terrible.

KALLIAS: I agree. It is inhuman.

ISMENE: How did the two women react?

DEBORAH: The second woman (the actual mother) turned to the King, because her compassion was aroused for her son, and said: "Please my Lord, give her the living child and do not kill it!"[50]

OEDIPUS AND KALLIAS (in unison): This is the woman who truly loved the infant. She is the true mother.

ISMENE: What did the other mother say?

---

47. I Kings 3:23.
48. I Kings 3:22.
49. I Kings 3:27.
50. I Kings 3:26.

DEBORAH: The first woman said: "Neither mine nor yours shall he be. Cut!"[51]

OEDIPUS AND KALLIAS IN UNISON: This is terrible. This is very selfish.

ISMENE (to OEDIPUS AND KALLIAS): This is the way the two of you have been acting: like this first woman.

ALEC: How did Solomon decide?

DEBORAH: The King spoke up and said: "Give the second woman the living child, and do not kill it, for she is his mother!" All of Israel heard the judgment that the King had judged. They had great awe for the King, for they saw that the wisdom of God was within him to do justice. The woman was rightfully awarded custody of her son.[52]

ISMENE (to OEDIPUS AND KALLIAS): This is the way the two of you have been acting. I feel like the baby in the story and the two of you would rather kill me than share me. Neither of you listens to me at all.

KALLIAS (to ISMENE): How do I not listen to you? Do you not love me?

ISMENE: Yes, I love you. But can you not understand I cannot leave my father. I am all he has.

KALLIAS: Why do I have to pay the price?

ISMENE (angrily): Pay the price? No one is asking you to pay any price. Go to Hades.

OEDIPUS (to ISMENE): How do I not listen to you, my daughter?

51. I Kings 3:26.
52. I Kings 3:27–28.

ISMENE (frustrated): Don't you understand that I love Kallias?

OEDIPUS: Are you going to leave me to be alone again?

ISMENE (throwing her hands up): No, father I won't leave you alone.

KALLIAS (to ISMENE): So I will leave the picture.

ISMENE (frustrated): No, this is not what I want either.

SOPHOCLES: I think we are at an impasse.

NATHAN (intervening, to DEBORAH): Deborah, you had told us in the last class that you had several biblical stories you would tell us. What is the other one?

DEBORAH: The story of Ruth and Naomi.

ALEC: Can you tells us this story, esteemed prophetess?

DEBORAH: The story begins when Naomi, her husband, and their two sons leave Judah to reside in Moab. a foreign land.[53]

ALEC: Why?

DEBORAH: Because food was scarce.

OEDIPUS (to NATHAN): Is this not where we were, Judah?

NATHAN: Yes, We were in Judah which is called Judea in Greek. Please continue, Deborah.

DEBORAH: Naomi's husband dies.

KALLIAS: How sad. And Naomi and her sons are in a strange land.[54]

53. Ruth 1:1–2.
54. Ruth 1:3.

DEBORAH: Yes, they are in strange land.

OEDIPUS: So, what happens?

DEBORAH: After the death of her husband, Naomi's two sons marry women of Moab, named Orpah and Ruth.

ISMENE: So, Naomi is all set.

DEBORAH: No. Naomi's two sons also die.[55]

ISMENE: How horrible. What does Naomi do?

DEBORAH: Naomi sets out to return to Judah, where, she has heard, food is no longer scarce.

ISMENE: Do her daughters-in law come with her?

DEBORAH: Naomi is accompanied by her two daughters-in-law at first; but at some point Naomi blesses her daughters-in-law and tells them to remain in Moab with their own people.

ISMENE: Do her daughters leave her?

DEBORAH: Both daughters-in-law weep, insisting that they will return with their mother-in-law to Judah. But Naomi again urges them to go, saying that she is too old to have more sons for them to marry.

ISMENE: Do they leave Naomi?

DEBORAH: Orpah kisses her mother-in-law and departs.

ISMENE: And Ruth?

DEBORAH: No, but Ruth will not leave her mother-in-law. In a moving speech, Ruth expresses her devotion to Naomi as a person, rather than as just a producer of sons for her.

55. Ruth 1:4–5.

ISMENE: What does Naomi say?

DEBORAH: And Ruth said, "Entreat me not to leave you, or to turn back from following after you; for wherever you go, I will go; and wherever you lodge, I will lodge; your people shall be my people, and your God, my God. Where you die, will I die, and there will I be buried. The Lord do so to me, and more also, if anything but death parts you and me." [56]

KALLIAS: This is really beautiful.

ISMENE (*angrily*): So why can't you see this is how I feel towards my father?

KALLIAS: He wants you for himself.

NATHAN: Go on, esteemed Deborah.

DEBORAH: This beautiful reciprocity continues throughout the story: Ruth worked very hard in the fields to provide enough barley to sell and to keep some for her and Naomi.

OEDIPUS (to ISMENE): As you have looked after me, dearest daughter.

DEBORAH: After the harvest, Naomi encouraged Ruth to meet her kinsman Boaz on the threshing floor and to lie down at his feet when he was done working.

NATHAN: And?

DEBORAH: When Boaz woke and noticed Ruth he blessed her for her kindness and noble character. "It has been fully reported to me, all that you have done for your mother-in-law since the death of your husband" [57]

---

56. Ruth 1:16-17.
57. Ruth 2:11.

ALEC: Boaz then gave Ruth six measures of barley for her to take home to Naomi.

DEBORAH: And Naomi unselfishly continues to look out for Ruth's welfare.

OEDIPUS (to ISMENE): As I have tried to do with you.

ISMENE (sadly): Even if it means giving up the man whom I love?

NATHAN: Please go on with the story, Deborah. How does Naomi continue to look after her daughter-in-law's interests?

DEBORAH: Naomi does her best to enhance Ruth's self-esteem, and she instructs Ruth about how to approach her kinsman Boaz.

NATHAN: How does this come about?

DEBORAH: Ruth worked very hard in the fields to provide enough barley to sell and to keep some for her and Naomi. After the harvest, Naomi encouraged Ruth to meet Boaz on the threshing floor and to lie down at his feet when he was done working. When Boaz woke and noticed Ruth he blessed her for her kindness and noble character. Boaz then gave Ruth six measures of barley for her to take home to Naomi.

NATHAN: Does the story end here?

DEBORAH: No. Boaz went before his friends and elders to purchase the land that had belonged to Elimelech and was now Naomi's. He did this so that he could also acquire Naomi and Ruth. Boaz was now able to marry Ruth. Boaz and Ruth had a son named Obed and a grandson named Jesse who would be the father of our King David.

NATHAN: And then?

DEBORAH: The story continues. "And may he be to you a restorer of life and a nourisher of your old age; for your daughter-in-law, who loves you, who is better to you than seven sons, has borne him." Then Naomi took the child and laid him on her bosom and became a nurse to it. Also, the neighbor women gave him a name, saying, "There is a son born to Naomi." And they called his name Obed. He is the father of Jesse, the father of David. [58]

ALEC: If I might say so, I think the story provides a way out of your dilemma, Ismene.

ISMENE: What is this way, Alec?

ALEC: Why can't you marry Kallias and have your father Oedipus live with you?

SOPHOCLES: Out of the mouth of babes.

ISMENE (to KALLIAS): Could you accept this, Kallias?

KALLIAS: I think so.

OEDIPUS: I also think so.

DEBORAH: So, we have a solution.

KALLIAS (to OEDIPUS): May I have the hand of your daughter in marriage? Will you be a father to me?

OEDIPUS (crying): Yes. Will you be a son to me?

KALLIAS (to Ismene): Will you marry me, Ismene?

ISMENE: Yes, with all my heart.

OEIDIPUS (coming to embrace them both): God bless you, my children.

58. Ruth 4:15-17

KALLIAS: Thank you, father.

NATHAN: I think it is time for a celebration.

DEBORAH: May I first briefly tell you one additional story?

NATHAN: Yes, of course.

DEBORAH: Do you remember that God sent a great flood to the world?

NATHAN: Yes.

SOPHOCLES: Why did your god do this?

NATHAN: Because He was disgusted over man's immorality.

DEBORAH: Do you remember what happens after the great flood that God sends recedes?.

NATHAN: Yes, God places a rainbow in the sky as the symbol to Noah and his descendants that there will be no more floods.[59]

DEBORAH: It is a symbol of hope in the future

SOPHOCLES: This is so different than the story of our first woman Pandora who looses all the evils into the world from the urn that Zeus has given her. Except for hope, which she keeps locked up in her urn and unavailable to humankind.[60]

NATHAN: Why did Zeus do this?

HESIOD: This was Zeus's punishment for Prometheus stealing fire for man.

SOPHOCLES: Yes, Zeus wanted to keep man dependent and was concerned that knowledge of fire would make him free.

KALLIAS: We must add these stories to Oedipus's class.

---

59. Genesis 6-9
60. Hesiod, *Theogony*, ll. 533-615; *Works and Days*, ll. 53-10.

ISMENE: Let us embrace hope.

NATHAN: We must. Now let us celebrate.

ALEC (for all the students): Yes, let us celebrate!

Scene II-15. Five years later Ismene has married Kallias and Oedipus lives with them. She has given birth to a son, Jason, who is now four years old and whom Oedipus dotes over. Sophocles, Kallias and Alec arrives to announce that Oedipus's course will become part of the standard curriculum for all students of Thebes and adjoining cities.

OEDIPUS: How was your day, my *engonos* (grandson)?

JASON: I played and read a little, *pappoulli* (grandfather).

OEDIPUS: What did you read, Jason?

JASON: I read about the cosmos, *pappoulli* Oedipus. About the creation of the world.

OEDIPUS: I think some of these stories are very dark, *engonos*.

JASON: Why, *pappoulli* Oedipus?

OEDIPUS: Because the way they look at life may not always be so positive, dearest *engonos*.

JASON: Would you like me to read another book?

OEDIPUS: Yes, grandson. Perhaps you should read this book. Look at the book by my chair, Jason.

JASON: What is this book, *pappoulli*?

OEDIPUS: It is a called a Septuagint, which is a Greek translation of a book from Judea.

JASON: What is this book from Judea, *pappoulli?*

OEDIPUS: They call it a *Torah* and it is written in Hebrew and Aramaic, two languages spoken in Judea.

JASON: Don't people speak Greek there?

OEDIPUS: No, my *engonos,* they speak Hebrew and Aramaic.

JASON: What is Judea? Where is it?

OEDIPUS: A land across the Mediterranean sea.

JASON: Have you been there, *pappoulli?*

ISMENE (entering the room, laughing): Oh yes, Jason, *pappoulli* has been in Judea.

JASON: Have you been there, *mitera* (mother)?

ISMENE (smiling): Oh yes, Jason, I have been there.

Sophocles, Kallias and Alec come bursting into the room.

KALLIAS: We have wonderful news.

ISMENE: What is it?

KALLIAS: Dear father, your class has been chosen as the top class in all of Thebes and the surrounding towns.

OEDIPUS (excitedly) : I can't believe it. What does this mean?

ALEC: It means that your ideas of how to live and how to overcome fatalism (*moira*)will be taught all over Greece.

JASON: I am so proud of you, *pappoulli* Oedipus.

OEDIPUS: I am proud of myself, *engonos* Jason. I am finally happy.

They all embrace.

THE END

www.ingramcontent.com/pod-product-compliance
Lightning Source LLC
Chambersburg PA
CBHW050410030726
47503CB00006B/2121